IN YOUR ROOM

JORDANNA FRAIBERG

razOr
bill

In Your Room

RAZORBILL

Published by the Penguin Group
Penguin Young Readers Group
345 Hudson Street, New York, New York 10014, U.S.A.
Penguin Group (USA) Inc., 375 Hudson Street, New York, New York 10014, U.S.A.
Penguin Group (Canada), 90 Eglinton Avenue East, Suite 700, Toronto, Ontario,
Canada M4P 2Y3 (a division of Pearson Penguin Canada Inc.)
Penguin Books Ltd, 80 Strand, London WC2R 0RL, England
Penguin Ireland, 25 St Stephen's Green, Dublin 2, Ireland
(a division of Penguin Books Ltd)
Penguin Group (Australia), 250 Camberwell Road, Camberwell, Victoria 3124,
Australia (a division of Pearson Australia Group Pty Ltd)
Penguin Books India Pvt Ltd, 11 Community Centre, Panchsheel Park, New Delhi—
110 017, India
Penguin Group (NZ), 67 Apollo Drive, Rosedale, North Shore 0632, New Zealand
(a division of Pearson New Zealand Ltd.)

Penguin Books (South Africa) (Pty) Ltd, 24 Sturdee Avenue, Rosebank,
Johannesburg 2196, South Africa

Penguin Books Ltd, Registered Offices: 80 Strand, London WC2R 0RL, England

10 9 8 7 6 5 4 3 2 1

Library of Congress Cataloging-in-Publication Data

Fraiberg, Jordanna.
  In your room / by Jordanna Fraiberg.
    p. cm.
  Summary: Teens Molly and Charlie connect through email when their
complicated families exchange houses for the summer, but a misunderstanding
threatens the emerging relationship just when the two are about to secretly meet.
  ISBN 978-1-59514-193-4
  [1. Home exchanging—Fiction. 2. Long-distance relationships—Fiction.
3. Fashion design—Fiction. 4. Bicycles and bicycling—Fiction. 5. Email—Fiction.
6. Stepfathers—Fiction. 7. Lesbians—Fiction. 8. Boulder (Colo.)—Fiction.
9. Los Angeles (Calif.)—Fiction.] I. Title.
  PZ7.F8436In 2008
  [Fic]—dc22
                                    2007051688

Printed in the United States of America

For Alex

JUNE

From: Charlie
To: Molly
Date: June 15, 2008 12:05 A.M. PST
Subject: In your room

Dear Molly:

My name is Charlie and I'm staying in your house for the summer. More precisely, I'm staying in your room.

Anyway, I'm writing because your cat showed up on the windowsill about ten minutes ago and hasn't stopped meowing since. He won't come in or drink or anything, so I figured you might be familiar with this behavior and know what to do. Or maybe he's just freaking out because you're gone. If you have any tips on what to do, that'd be great. Thanks. Hope you're liking our house so far (if you've even arrived yet).

Charlie

From: Molly
To: Charlie
Date: June 15, 2008 9:00 A.M. MST
Subject: Re: In your room

___

Dear Charlie:

OMG! I forgot to leave a note about the cat! I hope he didn't keep you up all night. He's not even mine—he technically belongs to this old man down the street, but he spends most of his time outdoors, seducing suckers like me for attention, so he comes by a lot. You can just give him a piece of cheese to stop the meowing. . . . It always calms him down and seems to be the only thing he'll eat. And don't worry if you hate cats or anything—he's totally harmless. I don't know his real name so I just call him Cheese (not that original, I know) and he seems to respond, but I guess he'd respond to anything if it meant he got his chin scratched (and a piece of cheese). He'll probably leave eventually if you close the window, but I can't promise, since I always let him in. Hope that helps!

Molly

TWO WEEKS EARLIER

1

Throw your dreams into space like a kite, and you do not know what it will bring back, a new life, a new friend, a new love.

—Anaïs Nin

Molly Hill closed her eyes and took a deep breath, trying to contain a sniffle.

"Need some tissue?" Celeste whispered, reaching into her purse.

Molly shook her head no. She had promised herself she wouldn't cry no matter how much she wanted to. She knew she was supposed to be happy for the bride and that she needed to put her own feelings aside. But she couldn't. Not when this wedding meant that her life was about to change too. Not when it was her own mother up there at the altar, exchanging the "for better or for worses" and the "I dos."

As the rabbi pronounced the couple husband and wife, Rina reached over and squeezed Molly's hand, but it was too late. The tears had already started. Celeste took hold of her other hand and leaned in closer.

Laura had wanted Molly up there next to her under the chuppah, but there was no way Molly could handle trying to keep her emotions under

uch safer sitting in the front

one of the most important

real right to be upset. Her

nd Laura had pretty much

hs before. She had devoted

e now got another chance at

Ron was this globe-trotting

en married, and was the last

with? Who was she to judge

before going off to college?

y, a year was starting to feel

ned the happiest smile she

ast on their way back down

e squeezed her way through

ir regards to the newlyweds

erlooking the Pacific. Molly

water. They only lived about

fifteen miles from the ocean, but it felt more like a hundred in Los Angeles traffic. She wasn't much of a beach girl anyway.

"Take this," Celeste insisted, appearing next to her. She handed Molly a glass of champagne.

"I'm okay," Molly said, refusing the drink. "Seriously."

"I don't believe you, but this should definitely not go to waste," Celeste said, taking a sip.

"I'm really proud of you," Rina said, staring out at the view next to

Molly. "I know how hard this day is for you, and it's really impressive that you've kept it from your mom, but you don't have to hide it from us."

Molly could always count on Celeste to lighten the mood and on Rina to say just the right thing to make her feel less alone. "I don't know what I'd do without you guys," she said, wrapping an arm around each of them. "You have to promise to keep me busy this summer. I don't know how much newlywed bliss I can handle."

"I don't think keeping you busy is gonna be a problem, Miss 'I have the next ten years already scheduled,'" Celeste teased, nudging Molly.

"I'm not that bad! Aren't you going to back me up?" Molly asked, turning to Rina.

"I think it's great," Rina said. "You know what you want, and you're going after it."

"Exactly. I'm just focused," Molly said, addressing Celeste. "You'll see—when I become a huge designer, you're going to be begging me for free clothes."

"Well, veering a little from the plan isn't such a bad thing," Celeste said, as Laura and Ron appeared on the terrace, which had already filled with the rest of the guests. "It worked out pretty well for your mom."

It was easy for Celeste to say. She was always the type to leap before looking first, no matter the consequences. Molly figured she was like that because of her dad. He'd walked out on Celeste and her mom when Celeste was five and had been in and out of her life ever since. All of Celeste's impulsive behavior was probably a play for his attention.

Molly had lost her dad too, but that was different. When he died, she knew he was never coming back. There was no confusion—and no one's attention to compete for.

Once everyone had settled with their champagne and shrimp cocktail, Ron clinked his glass to quiet the crowd. Molly glanced around the room at the smiling guests with their eyes trained on the happy couple, and had the sinking feeling that things were only going to get worse. But then again, she never was one to trust her instincts.

Still having difficulty with the whole stepdad-ness of it all, Molly grabbed Celeste's drink out of her hand. No matter that it was lipstick-stained and half empty. At that moment Molly was a glass-half-empty kind of girl.

"I would like to thank everyone for joining us here on this very special occasion," Ron began. "As you all know, I have every reason to celebrate. I never thought I would find a woman as beautiful, loving, and compassionate as Laura. But I have another reason to be grateful. And her name is Molly. I have always wanted a daughter. I am so proud to call Molly mine. And now, to kick-start our family, Molly will be joining us on our honeymoon!"

"What?!" Molly yelped, louder and with less grace than she would have liked. Her stomach lurched into her throat.

"That's right," her mother joined in. "We're all going to Boulder, Colorado, for the summer. Surprise! We're doing a house swap."

• • •

Charlie Richards gave his bike one last push. He rounded the corner onto his street and coasted the rest of the way to his house, turning his iPod up to full volume. His parents were paranoid about him listening to music when he was on his bike, and he usually kept it at a low volume so he could hear the traffic, but he drew the line at their quiet, tree-lined street. There was something about the surrounding mountains and the peaceful pocket of Boulder suburbia, something majestic that begged for a chorus. Besides, he knew every driveway, doorway, and intersection like the back of his hand and could navigate the way blind. He did just that sometimes—closed his eyes—when the moment was right.

Summer was his favorite time of year in Boulder. Most people flooded the area in the winter months to ski or snowboard, which Charlie also loved, but the real magic was in the summer, when the area's hidden beauty came out.

Charlie sailed up the driveway and in through the garage. He hoisted the bike over his shoulder and hung it on an empty hook next to a series of other bikes. To the layman, they were all the same, but to Charlie they each had their distinct purpose: thicker wheels for rougher terrain, thinner ones with lighter frames for greater speed, and so on. A row of women's bikes dangled from the adjacent wall, including two identical child-size pink ones.

All the ski and snowboarding paraphernalia was in the back, half-obscured by boxes, in hibernation until the next snow.

He slowly opened the door into the house to avoid making any noise. He had gone for a ride after school and discovered a new trail, which meant he was now almost an hour late for dinner. He could hear voices in the kitchen but needed to run up to change before anyone realized he was home. There would be even more hell to pay if he showed up at the table with mud splattered all over him.

"Charlie? Is that you?" a woman's voice called out.

He winced. Busted. "I'll be right in," he yelled back from halfway up the stairs. "Just need to wash my hands."

"Do it in here."

He did an about-face and sheepishly entered the kitchen. "Sorry I'm late."

His eleven-year-old twin sisters, Mia and Heather, and his two moms, Sally and Lisa, were sitting around the table, already on dessert. Lisa was Charlie's biological mother, but those kinds of technical distinctions were frowned upon in their household. To enforce that point, everyone's legal last name was Richards, which, technically speaking, was Sally's name to begin with. Charlie was happy with that decision if for no other reason than he didn't have to go through life as Charlie Babcock—Babcock being Lisa's maiden name.

"Don't worry about it," Lisa said, removing a plate from the oven and putting it on the table. "I kept this warm for you."

"What's going on?" Charlie asked, suspicious that neither of his moms, particularly Sally, seemed remotely annoyed that he was so late. They were used to it since he was prone to losing track of time on the trails, but that didn't mean they liked it.

"It's a family meeting," Mia, the blonder and slightly smaller of the sisters, said.

"Everything's okay," Sally said, reading the look on Charlie's face. "We just wanted everyone here so that we could let you know our summer plans."

"Yay!" the twins said in unison.

"We have a fantastic surprise. We've decided that we're all going to Los Angeles for the summer," Lisa announced.

"L.A.? What do you mean?" Charlie asked over his sisters' high-pitched squeals of delight. He turned to Sally. "I thought just you were going for a month." Sally was a pediatric oncologist and had a teaching fellowship at the Children's Hospital there.

"That was the plan," Lisa started to explain, "but I got a call from one of my grad school colleagues this morning who asked if I was interested in taking over his summer courses at UCLA. When he told me that he was coming out here with his family for the summer, we realized we could just swap homes."

"A house swap?" Charlie asked with a hint of disdain.

"It's when you trade your house with someone else's," Heather chimed in.

"Yeah, I get the concept," he snapped. "Can't I just stay here with Dan or someone?"

"Nooo!" Mia howled in protest.

"You can't do that," Heather added. "You have to stay with us."

"We're sorry, honey," Lisa said. "We don't want to split up the family for that long."

"But what about my company?" Charlie knew that was a losing argument. He didn't have a company so much as a strategy to make money over the summer leading mountain bike tours. "I've already started posting fliers."

"I'm sure your customers will understand," Sally said. "You can pick it up again when we get back in August."

He could have sat there and drawn out the conversation for another hour, but there was no point. As much as his parents told him he was free to explore who he was and to express his opinions, at seventeen he still had no real say, and the decision had clearly already been made. They were going to Los Angeles. But why, *why* did it have to be there? He could handle a city like Portland or Seattle and would probably not have cared all that much if that were the plan. But L.A. stood for everything he hated: freeways, SUV traffic jams, the worst air quality in the country, to say nothing of the rampant materialism, and, of course, *Hollywood*. It was a city that had nothing to offer, and the next two months were going to be a big waste of time.

"What about Park City?" he asked. "Do I have to give that up too?" His best friend, Dan, was spending the summer at his rich uncle's lodge in the mountains and had invited Charlie up for a weekend in August.

"I don't see any reason why you couldn't still go," Sally said, looking over at Lisa.

"Fine with me too," Lisa said.

Charlie rose from the table. There was nothing more to be said. He didn't feel the need to thank them for not ruining his entire summer.

He left the room, headed back through the garage, and took one of the bikes off the rack on his way out.

Your sacred space is where you can find yourself again and again.

—Joseph Campbell

"Hey there, Cheesy," Molly said to the meowing gray cat on her windowsill. "Are you going to come in and keep me company?"

She was sitting on the white shag rug in the middle of her room, surrounded by mounds of clothes and the open drawers of the flower-painted dresser she had just emptied to make room for the arriving guests. She was usually very organized, especially when it came to travel, and would normally have all her clothes stacked in neat piles days before departure. But that was when she was looking forward to something—a vacation or a visit with relatives. This was something else entirely. Something she preferred to pretend wasn't happening. But now that they were leaving in the morning, she had to acknowledge the reality of the months ahead and finally pack.

"That's my little guy." The cat sauntered up and planted himself in her lap as she sorted through the mess around her. "You think this house swap is the dumbest thing ever, don't you?" she said, scratching the folds of loose fur beneath his chin. The cat let out a steady stream of purring. "Yeah, that's right. I do too."

A few remnants of Molly's childhood dotted the room: a once-abundant stuffed animal collection lined the top of the bookcase and was only visible if she was lying in bed; a now-dilapidated dollhouse Laura had commissioned for Molly after her father died jutted out from a nook in the back of the room. In its heyday, it boasted pristine yellow paint on the exterior and every luxury within, from intricate china-patterned dishware to Jacuzzi tub bathrooms and a giant playroom with every toy imaginable. Most of these items had long since been lost or destroyed, but Molly couldn't bring herself to get rid of the house or even remove it from her room.

But more than anything, the room resembled the studio of a budding designer. The bookshelves were lined with four years of *Vogue* and *Teen Vogue* back issues, as well as various books on fashion, photography, and art. A bare canvas dress form stood in the corner by the back window with multicolored pins protruding from it at every angle. It stood next to Molly's prized possession, a 1978 Singer sewing machine she'd inherited from her grandmother. It stood on a table of its own in the corner of the room near the far left window so that Molly could see the street below while she worked. Sketches, both rough and complete, of dresses, skirts, shirts, and pants were posted on a bulletin board propped against the wall behind it, some with corresponding Polaroids of the finished products tacked below.

Her grandmother's vanity, aligned against the right wall, displayed her perfumes and makeup, what little she had, and what Molly liked to call her "snapshot of life"—a giant corkboard collage of her friends, mainly of Rina and Celeste, and inspirational magazine cutouts—covered half of the back wall by the door so that every day Molly went to sleep and woke up looking at it.

"It's not like the Arctic, you know," Celeste announced, barging into the room. She had grown up across the street but had probably spent more time in Molly's bedroom than her own.

Molly continued sorting through her winter sweaters, deciding which ones to take. "Well, there's snow there all year long. I've seen it on the Weather Channel."

Celeste rolled her eyes and made a beeline for the closet. "That's only at the top of the mountains at, like, fifty thousand feet or whatever. And we both know you won't be making any treks up there."

Celeste's supermodel-thin body, long, wavy blond hair, and perma-tan made her a Cali girl through and through. Molly had long accepted the fact that when she was with Celeste, boys would never pay her any notice, or if they did, it would be as a result of an ill-conceived plan that Molly could get Celeste to like them. Molly had also tacitly accepted the fact that her shoulder-length black hair, almost-as-black eyes, and pale skin were not the prototype for female beauty, especially in Los Angeles.

A few minutes later Rina arrived. "I've been trying to get here forever but my mom made me sit through dinner with the Singhs, which makes absolutely no sense since we're about to spend the next six weeks in India with them, starting with a very long plane ride in two days." She plunked herself down on the floor next to Molly and began sorting through her discarded piles. "Ugh. Don't even ask how I'm going to survive."

Molly had been friends with Rina since freshman year when they were partners in biology. Rina was the definition of an old soul and understood Molly's thoughts without needing much explanation. Celeste, on the other hand, was only interested in talking about one thing: boys.

Celeste emerged from the closet wearing a red summer dress. She adjusted the mirror hanging on the back of the closet door to get a better view of her backside. "Can I borrow this for the summer?"

"No way," Molly said, transferring a neat stack of notebooks on the floor next to her bed to a box labeled JUNIOR YEAR.

"Oh, come on! You're clearly leaving all your best stuff behind for a reason."

"I'm all too aware of what happens to clothes you borrow."

"And what's that?" Celeste asked innocently.

"They disappear forever."

Celeste smirked. "Okay. A proposition. I only borrow one item at a time and return it to your closet before taking something else. Like Netflix."

"It's not like I have any way of knowing if you're lying all the way from Boulder."

"You have my word. And besides, I can be your spy to make sure nothing is out of place or stolen with the aliens living here."

"Okay, fine. One item at a time, including belts," Molly conceded. Half her wardrobe would likely be missing or ruined by the time she came back. "But you can't use your key. Even if they are aliens, they still deserve a little privacy."

"Aren't you bringing this?" Rina asked, holding up a purple folder. In it was the application for a coveted fall internship with Cynthia Vincent, Molly's favorite designer.

"I changed my mind," Molly said, putting the folder back on the desk. She had been working on her application for the last month and had been planning on spending the summer finalizing her sketches, shopping for fabric, and making one of the dresses in her portfolio before the August first deadline. She had also been planning on accomplishing all this in the place where she was most creative—her room. It seemed stupid, but she didn't feel like she could pull it off in some strange house, in a strange city, with none of her usual materials or resources at her disposal. "I need my own things around me to be able to focus."

"You never know how you'll feel when you get there," Rina suggested, slipping the folder into Molly's laptop bag. "Take it. Just in case."

"Well, if you're not working, it will at least give you more time to get to know some Boulder boys," Celeste said.

"Right. I'm so glad my social calendar is wide open," Molly snorted.

Celeste *tsk*ed. "You'll never get a bearded mountain man with that attitude."

Molly shook her head. Celeste could never last for more than a month without being lavished with attention by at least one suitor. For Molly, it wasn't that simple. "You're not exactly one to talk. This is the longest you've been single since the fifth grade."

"Precisely!" Celeste said. "Which is why I'm going to seduce some unsuspecting hottie after you guys both abandon me for the summer."

Rina laughed. "And we have no doubt you'll succeed. Multiple times."

Molly envied Celeste's ability to not only fall in love but to fall out of it just as quickly. She was immune to the perils of heartache and turned any breakup into an opportunity to meet someone else. Celeste believed that the key to happiness was to never look back. Molly didn't have all that much to look back on except for a hopeless yearlong crush on Jacob Miller that had culminated in a single date at the end of freshman year, right before he went away to summer camp. He had kissed her on the cheek and told her he'd see her in August. Molly spent the next six weeks reliving that kiss—her first—and imagining all the *real* kissing they'd be doing when he got back.

Only Jacob had never called or responded to her e-mails, and she'd had to wait until the first day of school to find out that he was already dating someone else.

She hadn't liked anyone since. If love hurt so much before she even got a chance to experience it, she couldn't imagine how bad it would feel to get her heart broken for real.

"Well, I say you're going to be a famous designer with or without the internship. And going to Boulder's your chance to stir things up," Celeste said, parading in front of the mirror in her newly borrowed red dress. "You'll see. This summer is going to be great. Now finish packing."

• • •

"You almost packed?" Lisa called out from down the hall. She was in Charlie's sisters' room, getting things organized for the trip.

People often asked if it was confusing having two moms, as in, did he ever get them mixed up, which he thought was a really dumb question. In fact, he got asked that more about his moms than he did about his sisters, who were actually twins, and he certainly didn't have any trouble telling Mia and Heather apart.

"Getting there," he yelled back. He was lying on top of his unmade bed, tossing a baseball and watching it arc up and barely graze the ceiling before spinning back down and landing in his glove. He'd gotten both the ball and glove as a birthday present from his paranoid great-uncle whom he'd never met, but who always sent Charlie sports-related gifts to make sure he was exposed to enough "guy things."

"I can hear the ball. That means you're not packing."

"Fine," he droned. It was amazing the way his mom had supersonic hearing when she needed it. He slid the ball and glove beneath the bed and got up to survey the room. It was a mess: piles of clean and dirty clothes were strewn across the floor, half the sheets hung off the bed exposing the mattress, and books were scattered everywhere. The poster of Adam Craig, his favorite mountain bike rider, was torn and starting to curl at the corners, but Charlie wasn't prepared to let it go.

He hauled a beat-up blue-and-yellow duffel bag out of the closet, dragging with it a few dust bunnies, several magazines, and a book on the history of mountain biking. He scooped the clothes off the floor and dumped them in the bag, figuring that if he'd worn them recently they were good enough to wear all summer.

He sat down next to clear off his desk and unceremoniously swept the unused stack of fliers advertising his bike tours into the blue recycling bin next to his chair, accidentally knocking over a picture frame that had previously been obscured. He turned it over to the snapshot of him and Sylvia on their first date. Now that she was, as of two days ago, his *ex-*girlfriend, he unfastened the hooks, slid the velvet back off the frame, and removed the photo. Looking at it closely, he could see that even back then he wasn't that into her. He knew he should have trusted his instincts and not bothered going out with her. Had he paid a little more attention to this picture and all the other signs telling him to jump ship two months earlier, he would have saved himself a lot of trouble and not made an enemy out of her.

Charlie's cell rang and he snapped it open. "I'm on my way," he said preemptively. "Of course I'm not bailing."

He looked around at his now half-disheveled room. The rest of the packing could wait. "See you guys in ten."

"You're not staying for dinner?" Sally appeared in the hall holding a spatula, wearing the orange apron Charlie had given her a few birthdays ago.

"Can't. Dan and Teddy are already waiting," he said, opening the door to the garage.

"I know this is your last night with your friends, but try not to make it too late, okay? We want to get an early start."

"I won't." He wanted to leave before he got roped back in. It wasn't all the talk of clothes and girl stuff that he minded, living in an all-female house, but the power his moms, and even his sisters, often had over him. He was a sucker for a nice gesture and felt, as the only male figure in the house, the tug of obligation. When he was away from home he could just be himself.

• • •

Even at seven P.M., the sun was still high up in the sky, giving the impression it was never going to set. This was what he loved most about Boulder nights in the summer—the feeling of endless possibility. He released his hands out to the side like wings and closed his eyes, taking in the clean, crisp mountain air, and the summer sounds of sprinklers, mockingbirds, and mosquitoes.

Charlie heard the low hum of Central Park from over a block away. From that distance, the white lights embracing the trees around the garden sparkled like diamonds, even in the light of day. Charlie stopped pedaling so he could coast the rest of the way, enjoying the view for as long as possible.

As he reached the bike rack, the low hum turned into overlapping conversations. The party was in full effect. Several bars were set up on the perimeter, with tables scattered across the grassy middle. Slide 99, a local band comprised mainly of Fairview High alumni, performed on a stage at the back.

"Duuuuude!" a loud voice called.

Charlie turned around and saw Teddy and Dan surrounded by a group of girls on the grass.

"Come on over, bro!" Teddy yelled again. He had his arms draped around two of the girls, whom Charlie recognized from school. Freshmen, if he remembered correctly.

"What took you so long? We've been here for almost an hour," Teddy said when Charlie reached them.

"Hey, guys," Charlie said. "Sorry I'm late."

"Well, you're here now. Let the games begin," Dan said, greeting Charlie with a half-hug and a backslap.

Charlie, Dan, and Teddy had all met in ski school when they were five. They had been the three best in their age group and always found themselves down the slope first with time to spare while they waited for everyone else. The coach eventually hired an assistant for the stragglers so he could focus on the threesome, with the hopes of finding Olympic potential among them. They all ended up wasting away their talent, according to the coach—Charlie fell in love with mountain biking, Dan fell in love with soccer, and, by the age of ten, Teddy fell in love with girls.

"Dude, promise when you're in L.A., you'll go to a strip club and get a lap dance for me."

Charlie rolled his eyes, but Teddy pressed further. "Promise, dude," he said, holding his clenched fist out. "It's all I ask."

Unable to resist Teddy's charm, Charlie broke into a smile and punched it in.

"That's my boy. And keep track of the real-or-fake quotient. It'll keep you busy for hours in that city."

"What's real or fake?" one of the girls piped up.

"Here, let me show you," Teddy said, running at her, zombie style, with his arms extended, reaching for her chest.

"You're unbelievable," Charlie said, shaking his head and laughing while the girl playfully swatted Teddy away.

Another girl, a cute brunette, sidled up to Charlie. "I know you," she said, fake-punching his arm. "You're Charlie Richards."

"Oh, here it comes," Dan said.

"That I am," he responded, taking in her compact, slender build. She looked like a cheerleader. Too bad. Charlie wasn't in the mood to flirt. "Anyone need a drink?" he asked, trying to exit the situation as gracefully as possible.

"I'll come with you," Dan said.

"Wait up," Teddy called, leaving the girls behind. He turned Charlie around to face him. "Dude, she was totally into you. You'd better not be this picky in L.A."

Charlie shrugged. "You call it picky—I call it getting wiser with age." He never tried all that hard or gave much thought to his appearance, but for some reason girls were drawn to his floppy blond hair and lanky build. He was done, though, going out with someone just because she was cute and willing; it was a recipe for things ending badly.

"Incoming," Teddy alerted his friends. Charlie looked up to see a group of six kids—three girls and three boys—gliding through the crowd. And Sylvia—his ex—was among them. She was unmistakable, with her green eyes and ponytailed red hair that swung like a pendulum in the middle of her back. While she didn't make eye contact with Charlie, it was clear she knew he was there by the self-conscious way she pushed an imaginary hair away from her face and started to laugh.

"Maybe we should walk the other way," Dan suggested.

"No, I'm good," Charlie said, as the group approached.

"It's not you I'm worried about," Dan said.

"Walking away makes me an asshole."

"And not walking away invites a scene," Teddy said. "Dude, the girl's obsessed with you."

"Give her a little more credit," Charlie said. He had originally planned on letting things with Sylvia peter out through the summer, but when he'd found out he was going to L.A., it had seemed better to make a clean break. Sylvia hadn't seen it that way. She'd begged Charlie to give her another chance and forced him to admit that he didn't like her anymore.

It was true, but it had sounded much harsher out loud.

When she got closer, Charlie broke away from his friends to approach her. "Hi, Sylvia."

She walked right past, her eyes fixed ahead, like she didn't even see him.

He had expected her to blow him off, but he didn't want to be a jerk and ignore her too, especially after hurting her so much.

"All right, we can go now," he said, returning to Dan and Teddy.

"To the bar?" Teddy asked, raising his empty plastic beer cup.

Charlie surveyed the crowd in the middle of the park near the band. Everyone was drinking and dancing to the music, having what seemed like the time of their lives. If he were staying for the summer he would have been among them, probably even dancing with Sylvia, but he was no longer in the mood for a party. "You guys go ahead. I still haven't packed, and we're pretty much leaving at the crack of dawn."

"But this is our last night, dude," Teddy protested.

"I'll be back so fast you won't even know I was gone," Charlie said, breaking off in the other direction.

"Hey! Don't forget! I'll see you in Utah, bro!" Dan called out.

Charlie pumped his fist in the air in response and jogged off across the grass toward his bike.

He pedaled down the street away from the park, the music and chatter floating up into the dark sky behind him. A few blocks down he arrived at a gate with a sign that read CLOSED FROM SUNSET TO SUNRISE. He ignored it, slipping through an opening in the side. With no one else in his way and the moonlight guiding him, he made it up to a ridge in just fifteen minutes, followed it a few hundred feet, and then turned down a barely visible passage that had been formed by Charlie's use.

He charged down, full speed, anticipating every fallen branch and exposed root in his path. With no apparent deceleration, he made a sudden left onto another barely formed trail, which descended at a more gradual rate, until it ended at an outcropping of rocks.

Charlie got off his bike and propped it up against the bark of a nearby trunk. He pulled a small flashlight out of a side pocket near the rear wheel and pointed it to the right of the tree, revealing a makeshift passageway formed by a cluster of overlapping stones. He lowered his head and crouched through, entering a cave that extended almost ten feet in.

He sat down on a scattering of pine needles that covered the ground. They still smelled fresh even though they had been there for months. He shined the light out into the forest, exposing little treasures of the night: insects, nests, an owl. Charlie lay down with his hands folded behind his head and stared up at the roof of stone. Shards of moonlight shot down through the fault lines between the overhanging boulders, illuminating his foot, a few pine needles, spots of green lichen crawling over the surrounding rocks like a blanket. He had discovered the cave over two years before on one of his first exploratory rides through uncharted terrain. He returned regularly, especially when he needed time alone. It was the only place where the rest of the world dropped away.

After about an hour he got up, retrieved his bike, and followed another path down the rest of the mountain that eventually spilled out onto a street around the corner from his house. It was time to get back to reality.

3

What if I told you it was all meant to be / Would you believe me?

—Kelly Clarkson, "A Moment Like This"

"Rise and shine!" Celeste marched into Molly's bedroom carrying two large cups from Starbucks.

"This isn't happening." Molly pulled the covers over her head.

Celeste put down the tray and stripped the comforter from the bed. "It's just like ripping off a Band-Aid. The faster it happens, the sooner the pain is over."

"I like my pain," Molly said grumpily.

"Then have some of this." Celeste handed her a steaming cup of coffee. "Extra hot, the way you like it."

Molly took a sip, taking in Celeste's uncharacteristically disheveled appearance: baggy sweatpants, oversize hoodie, and slippers. "You actually woke up early to do this," she marveled. "You're really going to miss me, aren't you?"

"You think I can't handle a couple of months on my own? Please."

"I'm going to miss you more, if it makes you feel any better," Molly said.

She got up and changed into the jeans and T-shirt she had laid out at the foot of the bed the night before.

"Honey? You ready?" Laura called from downstairs. "The car's packed."

"Okay. I'll be right there."

"See? I did you a favor—otherwise you'd still be asleep. I'll help you take your stuff down," Celeste said, picking up one of the bags waiting by the door. "You coming?"

"I'll be right behind you," Molly said, straightening out the comforter and returning all the decorative pillows to the bed. She had changed the sheets before she went to bed and slept on top of them so she wouldn't have to deal with it now.

Once Celeste left the room, Molly sat down at her sewing machine and ran her fingers along the hard black surface before shrouding it with the patchwork cover she had made from scraps of spare fabric.

She looked around the room one last time before turning off the lights and closing the door behind her.

• • •

Charlie stood on the back bumper of the minivan and reached over the roof to fasten the strap on the bike rack. There was only space for two bikes, but he had managed to fit three by tying his sisters' bikes together, since they were so small. He had already loaded the van with their luggage, filling up two entire rows. It felt like they were packing up the entire house and never coming back.

"Can you give me a hand?" Sally came out balancing foldable beach chairs and various other items that had been shoved into a garbage bag at the last minute.

"I'm sure they have those in L.A.," Charlie said, helping her steady a falling chair. "And there's no more room."

"Of course there is," she said, sliding a chair under a row of seats. "See?"

"I still haven't put my bag in," he said. "But it's about a third the size of what you guys packed."

Mia and Heather were on the front lawn, taking turns doing somersaults and cartwheels, cheering each other on.

"It's six o'clock in the morning," he said, shaking his head as he walked past them on his way back into the house. "Why are you so awake?"

"Because we're excited!" Mia called back, but Charlie was already inside.

His duffel bag was sitting unzipped on his bed where he had left it when Lisa summoned him to pack the car earlier that morning. He grabbed a few loose items of clothing that were still scattered across the floor and shoved them in.

He scanned the room to make sure he wasn't forgetting anything else, when he noticed that he had left the picture of Sylvia lying faceup on his desk. He picked it up and looked at it one last time before shoving it in his top desk drawer.

He was about to leave when at the last second he decided to lock the drawer with the small gold key that normally dangled from the desk. He then took the key out and put it in an old Nike shoe box that was lying around. He had no idea who would be staying in his room for the summer, and he didn't really care, but there were some things he wanted to keep private.

He was just tall enough to reach the top of the bookcase, where he placed the shoe box, just out of sight, for safekeeping until he got back.

He zipped up his bag and walked out the door.

The longing for a destiny is nowhere stronger than in our romantic life.

—Alain de Botton, *On Love*

It was dark when they arrived, but the moonlight was bright enough to illuminate parts of the surrounding mountains. They were so close it felt like you could touch them, and there was no telling how high or wide they extended, the moon only allowing certain parts to be exposed at that hour.

"This is magnificent," Laura said in awe as they slid out of the car.

"Why don't you two go in and get settled. I'll unpack," Ron suggested.

"Don't be silly, honey, I'll help you. Molls, you go ahead and pick a room," Laura said, unlocking the front door and turning on the hall lights.

"I'll get that," Molly said, intercepting Ron as he removed her laptop from the trunk.

"Oh, sure, sorry." He handed it over. "State secrets?"

"Something like that." Molly awkwardly took the computer, juggling it a little before gaining control. *Why is it always* so *uncomfortable interacting with Ron?* she wondered.

The wood-cabin aroma that assaulted her when she walked down the front hall made it seem like they were moving into a sauna. Not surprising when every available surface seemed to be paneled.

The downstairs was basic: living room, dining room, kitchen. And the décor reflected the style, or lack thereof, of people who were too busy to care about material things, kind of like Ron's old apartment, which was a hodgepodge of secondhand furniture. Luckily, none of it had ended up in their house when he moved in. Whoever lived here still used a corded phone that sat atop a table in the front hall, like a relic from another era.

She made her way up the stairs and poked her head into the first room off the landing. Twin beds with matching pink comforters lined the back wall, which was also pink; two fuchsia beanbags slouched on the floor, and a long desk with two chairs faced the window. The desk's ivory surface peeked through the neat rows of sparkly stickers pasted on top. Had she been about five years younger, this room might have been a possibility, but there was no way she could bear reliving her "pink phase" for an entire summer.

Moving on, she discovered what was clearly a candidate for master bedroom: a queen-size bed, a simple vanity, a rocking chair with hand-knit throws folded on top, a wall of bookshelves, with the overflow stacked in semi-neat piles against all the remaining wall space, and a tattered Persian rug haphazardly tossed over the scratched hardwood floor.

A quick look through door number three revealed a home office with an antiquated desktop and more book piles. With one room left, Molly crossed her fingers. She hoped it would be a magical oasis, perfectly suited to her taste and needs. She tentatively opened the door to complete blackness. With the curtains drawn closed, not an ounce of moonlight entered the room. She pawed around, first on the wall to the right, then to the left, inching into the room, finally snagging her finger on a switch. The lights were the eco-friendly fluorescent kind, which had recently, because of Ron, appeared in her house as well. They lit up gradually like a dimmer in reverse. As the room glowed more brightly, Molly's summer fate was revealed—a full (thankfully not twin) bed, a desk, a dresser, and a few torn posters haphazardly tacked to the blue walls that still had masking tape stuck to the molding, left over from the last time it was painted. The room was devoid of any personality or style. *The guy who lives here must be a total bore,* she thought, standing in the middle of the room, taking it all in.

"Here you go." Ron appeared in the doorway, gripping her overstuffed suitcases in each hand.

"Oh, thanks. You can put them over here, I guess," she said, pointing to the floor by the dresser.

He brought them in and took a look around the room. "You okay in here?"

No, not really, she wanted to say, but that would only make things more awkward, since there was nothing either of them could do about it.

"Yup," she fibbed, "I'm good."

"Your mom's downstairs making hot chocolate. Want some?"

"I'm actually really tired, so can you tell her I'll see her in the morning?"

"Sure thing. Sleep well. We're just down the hall if you need us."

Molly felt a slight jab in her gut. *We?* She wasn't used to her mother being part of a "we" that didn't include her.

When Ron left she closed the door, stripped down to a T-shirt and underwear, turned out the lights, and ran across the room to the bed. Once settled, she turned on the lamp on the night table.

"No. Way," Molly said, peeling back the flattened navy blue comforter.

"NO. WAY." She got out of bed and pulled the comforter all the way back, revealing the sheets beneath, populated with various *Star Wars* characters, including the unbearable Jar Jar Binks.

Ugh! Thankfully it was warm enough that she didn't need anything covering her, so she smoothed the comforter back over the bed and lay down on top. It was just too weird sleeping in some strange guy's sheets, which for all she knew were still dirty. She wished she had thought about bringing her own.

She reached down for her computer bag by the bed and flipped open her laptop.

"Thank you, wireless," she exclaimed when the prompt appeared asking her if she would like to join the "actnow" wireless network, and moved her mouse to click yes.

"Please be online, please be online," Molly quietly repeated as she logged onto AOL instant messenger, hoping to see Celeste's name in her buddy list. She had a desperate need to vent, but Rina was on her way to India, and she knew there was basically no chance Celeste would be home on a Saturday night. She had to settle for e-mail instead.

From: Molly
To: Celeste
Date: June 14, 2008 10:33 P.M. MST
Subject: Star Wars sheets??????!!

C—FINALLY arrived but I'm sure you're at a party or even better, on some fabulous date. I'm sleeping in some boy's room with STAR WARS SHEETS!!! What is that? I mean, it's not like he's six or anything. Anyway, I don't really care why he has them, but I'm not going to sleep on them. I need my own and forgot to pack any! HELP!! Can you do me the hugest favor in the world and get me some from the closet in the hall . . . you know the one . . . a FULL set of white with lilac trim and whatever else you can find. I'll be so eternally grateful if you do this. And to show my thanks . . . you can keep the red dress for the whole summer. Oh! And while you're there, check out the aliens and find out if the boy is staying in my room and report back EVERY detail!!! I need to know what kind of nerd still sleeps in his ancient sci-fi-themed bedding. Love you lots and lots. The address is 227 Canyon View Road, Boulder, CO 80302. And please FedEx!! Don't think I can wait long enough for snail mail. Will pay you back of course.

xoxoxoxoxoxoxox

Molls

Molly hit send and closed her laptop. She turned out the lights and got up to open the curtains. "Wow," she said, looking up at the stars. She was unaccustomed to seeing those tiny, twinkling lights in smog-filled Los Angeles, especially not this many. She lay down on her back so she could look out the window.

With the light cast from the moon and stars, she could still make out the contours of the surrounding mountains. Some were in fact snowcapped, and, like Celeste had said, it seemed like they were fifty thousand feet high—too high for Molly to ever reach.

• • •

"Palm trees," Charlie said, as the minivan pulled into the driveway between two towering trunks. "I guess that means we're here."

"Palm trees don't even come from L.A.," Heather piped up on her way out of the car.

"How do you know that?" he asked, unfastening the straps on the bicycle rack.

"The Internet," she said, like it was obvious.

"You know what they say," he warned. "Don't believe everything you read."

"But this is true!" she insisted. "Everyone thinks they grow here, but they bring them in on trucks."

Charlie scoffed. Was *anything* about this place real? He helped Sally unpack while Lisa led the girls inside and got them settled.

"Let's deal with all this tomorrow," Sally said once the bags were in the house. "It's been a long day and we're all pooped."

"Good idea," Charlie said.

Lisa, having taken a tour of the house, directed Charlie to what was to be his room for the next two months.

"Sleep well," she said, kissing him good night. "I'll make a big breakfast in the morning and we can figure out what we're going to do."

"Sounds good, Mom." He turned around before going in and hugged her. He hadn't shown either of his parents much affection since they dropped the house swap bomb. But he knew they were trying, and it was about time he did too.

"Good night, kiddo."

Charlie pushed the door open wider and stepped in.

"What the . . . ?" He walked in farther to get a better look. "You've got to be kidding me!"

He had long ago come to terms with living in a girl-centric house, but he drew the line at sleeping in a girl's *room*. He paced the floor, taking in the delicate floral pattern on the comforter, the candles adorning every available surface, and, worst of all, the girl collage—a four-by-six-foot corkboard on one wall, papered with pictures of indistinguishable girls. The room reminded him of Sylvia's, as if there were a secret code to which all teenage girls adhered.

He went back out in the hall and counted the number of rooms—three, including the one he'd been assigned, and he noticed there weren't any downstairs. He opened the door to his sisters' room and went in.

"You didn't knock!" Mia called out from the dark.

He fumbled around and turned on the lights, revealing Mia and Heather lying in single beds divided by a nightstand, pushed against the back wall, evenly spaced between the windows. A small writing desk abutted the left wall, and a tall dresser on the right completed the furnishings. The room's décor was limited to a few etchings of birds and wildlife, and rows of old *National Geographic*s were stacked in the corner. Charlie would have taken this room any day, but the twin beds explained why it had been assigned to the girls. He was convinced, however, that once they got a peek at "his" room they would beg to switch, much preferring the opportunity to sleep surrounded by stuffed animals and collages.

But in the same moment he realized there was no way his moms would agree to the trade. They had been trying to encourage the girls to develop independent friends and interests, and separate beds were a major part of the effort.

Charlie sighed, turned off the lights, shut the door, and went back to "his" room. Everything seemed so clean, including the white rug that spread across the middle of the floor. The duffel bag he'd absentmindedly tossed on top of the cluster of white pillows neatly arranged on the bed suddenly looked dirtier and more ragged than ever. He looked down at his sneakers and noticed the dried mud still caked around them from his ride the night before. He would have preferred sleeping in the cave all summer than here, worrying about what he was going to stain or ruin.

Once he put the bag on the floor, the bed looked so inviting. He was at least psyched to sleep on such a huge mattress all summer. He kicked off his shoes and threw his clothes on the floor. Since he didn't know what to do about all the pillows, he just lay down on top of them. He expected it to feel weird and uneven but it was surprisingly comfortable.

"Meow."

He sat up and scanned the room. A cat? Did these people have a cat? No one had mentioned it, at least not that he could recall. He'd been paying so little attention, he didn't know anything much about the people who lived there.

"Meow."

He walked around, following the plaintive sound, and was led to the open window, where a plump gray cat sat on the other side. The cat greeted Charlie with another meow, this one less mournful, followed by a steady stream of purring when Charlie patted its head.

"Who are you, little guy?" Charlie asked. "How'd you get up here?" He leaned his head out the window, spotting the trellis of bougainvillea climbing the wall to the second-floor ledge.

"Want to come inside?" He tried to lure the cat in, but it wouldn't budge.

"Are you thirsty? Is that what's going on?" He took a half-finished Evian bottle from his backpack, emptied some change from a dish on the desk, and poured out water. He placed the dish on the sill but the cat ignored it and continued to squawk, staring right up at Charlie with its ice-blue eyes. "I'm not who you were expecting, am I?"

"Meow."

Charlie went over to the desk and found an old piece of mail to get the name of the girl who lived there. He then took out his laptop, got online, and did a Facebook search to find a way to contact her.

Since everyone was asleep and knew less about cats than he did, maybe Molly Hill could tell him what to do to please this fat little gray one.

From: Charlie
To: Molly
Date: June 15, 2008 12:05 A.M. PST
Subject: In your room

Dear Molly:

My name is Charlie and I'm staying in your house for the summer. More precisely, I'm staying in your room.

Anyway, I'm writing because your cat showed up on the windowsill about ten minutes ago and hasn't stopped meowing since. He won't come in or drink or anything, so I figured you might be familiar with this behavior and know what to do. Or maybe he's just freaking out because you're gone. If you have any tips on what to do, that'd be great. Thanks. Hope you're liking our house so far (if you've even arrived yet).

Charlie

From: Molly
To: Charlie
Date: June 15, 2008 9:00 A.M. MST
Subject: Re: In your room

Dear Charlie:

OMG! I forgot to leave a note about the cat! I hope he didn't keep you up all night. He's not even mine—he technically belongs to this old man down the street, but he spends most of his time outdoors, seducing suckers like me for attention, so he comes by a lot. You can just give him a piece of cheese to stop the meowing. . . . It always calms him down and seems to be the only thing he'll eat. And don't worry if you hate cats or anything—he's totally harmless. I don't know his real name so I just call him Cheese (not that original, I know) and he seems to respond, but I guess he'd respond to anything if it meant he got his chin scratched (and a piece of cheese). He'll probably leave eventually if you close the window, but I can't promise, since I always let him in. Hope that helps!

Molly

5

The meeting of two personalities is like the contact of two chemical substances: if there is any reaction, both are transformed.

—Carl Jung

"So how do you know the people who live here?" Molly hadn't been curious enough to ask the question until she woke up to Charlie's e-mail. It was weird knowing for certain that he was staying in her room, among the things that mattered most to her. Now that she was sure, she had to find out *something* about him.

"I went to graduate school with Lisa," Ron explained, adjusting the rearview mirror. They were on their way into town, Molly in search of a decent cup of coffee, and Ron on a grocery run while Laura unpacked. "Her partner's name is Sally and they have three kids. I think Charlie's around your age, and the girls must be at least ten by now."

Interesting, she thought. *Charlie has two moms.* "Do you see them a lot?"

"Usually just Lisa at conferences. I haven't seen Sally and the kids since the last time I was here, which was probably four or five years ago now."

So it was a dead end. Ron couldn't know much about Charlie, since it had been so long. And he probably wouldn't be able to tell her anything she hadn't already discerned from his bedroom.

"Why don't I drop you off to get your coffee and meet you back here in an hour?" he said, pulling over to the curb.

"Are you sure?" she asked, suddenly worried that she'd made her discomfort around him too obvious.

"You'll have a much better time here than looking for frozen peas in aisle five. There are a bunch of shops and cafés down that way," he said, pointing to a street that was blocked off to traffic. "It's Boulder's famous Pearl Street Mall."

"Oh. Okay, thanks," Molly said, getting out of the car. "I guess I'll see you in an hour."

Molly glanced around the mall. There was already quite a bit of activity on its brick-covered pedestrian walkway, even though it wasn't yet eleven on a Sunday morning. Street performers were arriving to reserve their turf, and restaurants were setting up their outdoor tables.

A hundred feet down the block, Molly spotted a coffee shop, with a sign that read BUBBA'S on the awning. She could also smell the distinct espresso aroma from the sidewalk and started to get her fix the moment she walked through the door.

The café had a cool, mellow vibe, with overstuffed lounge chairs, communal wood tables, and a magazine rack. It seemed like the kind of place where people hung out for hours late into the night, which maybe explained why it was empty at present.

Molly approached the counter to place her order, finding it abandoned too. She looked around, spotting a large message board with various announcements and fliers tacked on, and walked over to check it out. Much of it was covered with postings about rooms for rent, with a handful of massage therapists offering their services. Molly wondered what kind of person would choose their roommate in such a random way, or worse, allow some stranger from the lost-and-found of advertising into their house to rub smelly lotions into their skin. Gross.

Almost three-quarters of the way through the board, Molly read a posting that actually seemed interesting: "Salesperson needed for Second Time Around secondhand clothing store. 178 Pearl Street. Ask for Penelope."

Without thinking, Molly ripped the flier off the wall and stuffed it in her jeans pocket. Certain that she had broken the cardinal rule of public postings, she looked around to make sure no one had come in and seen her, then returned to the counter to wait. A few minutes later a redheaded girl around Molly's age came swinging through the employees-only door in the back, carrying a box of napkins. She had a coffee-stained apron over her T-shirt and cutoff jean shorts.

"Oh, jeez, you scared me!" the girl said, dropping the box on the counter when she finally noticed Molly standing there.

"I'm sorry," Molly said. "I thought you were open."

"We totally are. I just didn't hear you come in."

"Oh, good. I don't think I could last much longer without any caffeine."

"Tell me about it," the girl said. "I've had, like, three already. What can I get you?"

"Whatever's biggest and strongest."

"Late night?" she asked, pouring a cup.

"Something like that," Molly said. "We drove here and got in around midnight."

"Ah, a tourist. I'm surprised. I can usually spot them a mile away."

Molly smiled. "Well, I'm glad I'm not too obvious. I'm not really the outdoors type and you probably get a lot of those around here."

"So where you from?" the girl asked, handing Molly her coffee.

"Los Angeles," Molly said, reaching for her wallet.

"Huh. I'm Sylvia, by the way," the girl said, extending her hand.

"Nice to meet you," Molly said, shaking it. "I'm Molly. So how much do I owe you?"

"On the house," Sylvia insisted, waving away the money Molly was trying to hand her. "Welcome to the neighborhood."

"Thank you," Molly said, stuffing two dollars in the tip jar instead.

"Totally unnecessary," Sylvia said, walking Molly to the door. "How long are you here?"

"Until August."

"Well, I'm here all the time, so come by if you ever want to hang out," Sylvia offered. "Seriously, *all* the time."

Molly laughed. "Cool," she said on her way out. "Thanks. I will."

The bell on the café door tinkled behind her. Molly looked down at her watch. There was still almost half an hour until Ron returned for her, so she strolled down the street in search of the thrift store. She loved the vintage shops in L.A. and often perused them for design ideas. But she definitely wasn't looking for a job and had no idea what had compelled her to rip the flier off the wall. She could have just as easily memorized the address.

A couple of blocks down the street she found number 178. Had she not been looking for it, she never would have noticed it, let alone guessed that there was a clothing store behind the smudged windows and chipped wooden front door. A plump, gray-haired woman pushing sixty exited the store and tacked a "back in ten" note to the door frame.

"Murphy's law," she said with a chuckle when she turned around and saw Molly standing there. She took down the note and unlocked the door.

"Don't worry about it," Molly said, starting to back away. "I can come back another time."

"It's not a problem. Come on in," the woman said, opening the door. "Coffee can always wait."

Molly followed the woman, hoping she could do a quick drive-by of the racks and then be on her way.

"First time here, right?" the woman asked, leading Molly down the center aisle toward a desk at the back, where she dropped her purse. Racks of clothes spilled out on either side, three rows deep.

Molly nodded.

"Thought so. I never forget a face. Owned this place going on twenty years now. Sometimes I think it's what keeps my memory intact. My name's Penelope and I also have a pretty good head for inventory. Looking for anything special?"

Before Molly could answer, Penelope noticed the yellow flier she had posted at Bubba's peeking out of Molly's pocket. "Ah, you're here about the job."

"Well," Molly began, trying to think on her feet, "I guess I am."

Great. That was just great. Her mouth had a mind of its own, apparently.

"Fantastic," Penelope said, pulling an application from the desk. "As you can see, I'm short-staffed," she said, holding up the "back in ten" note.

"Thanks," Molly said, taking the application and tucking it in her back pocket next to the flier. "I'll bring it back."

"Nonsense! Fill it out here. It'll only take a minute." She reached behind her head and pulled a pen out of her hair, causing her bun to unravel, and handed it to Molly.

"Well, okay," Molly conceded. "But I have to be quick. I'm late. . . . " She was about to say what she was late for, but once again, she couldn't think fast enough to come up with a reason, so she left it at that. She was late. Molly leaned over the desk, refusing to sit down, filled out the form, and handed it back to Penelope, who stood watching her. She didn't look as old with her hair down, framing her face. "Here you go."

"Three-two-three area code, huh? That's . . . Los Angeles, correct?" Penelope muttered to herself while eyeballing the form. "No local number?" she asked, this time looking up at Molly.

"I just got here and don't know it yet. We're staying at a family friend's place. That's my cell, though," Molly explained, fidgeting.

"Well, I'll be in touch soon, Molly. I'd show you around the store, but I understand you're late."

"Yeah, thanks. I really do have to get going," Molly said, backing down the aisle toward the door.

"Boulder takes some getting used to," Penelope called out. "But once you do, you'll never want to leave."

Molly was about to explain that she hadn't moved to Boulder; she was just there for the summer. But she decided against it and instead smiled at Penelope before closing the door behind her.

Molly checked her e-mail as soon as she got home and there was a response from Celeste.

From: Celeste
To: Molly
Date: June 15, 2008 8:48 A.M. PST
Subject: Re: Star Wars sheets??????!!

Molls!! I miss u sooo much already. What am I going to do all summer without you? My mom just promised to take me on a shopping trip to Paris in August. Jealous? She just feels guilty that my dad flaked on me (again, long story) and that she has to deal with me now. So, any pillow talk with Han Solo? Don't worry, I'm going to march right on over (and ring the bell!) after Pilates and get you some decent sheets. I'll get the skinny on the aliens too. Any dirt on your end? Knowing you, you haven't done any snooping. Am I right? What are you waiting for? At the very least you deserve to rummage around the dork's room. And he's probably already peeked under your bed, so it's only fair, right? So get to it, and I expect a FULL report by the time I get home. Miss ya tons. Luv ya lots. Mean it.
C.

Celeste was right. Molly hadn't even thought about snooping around the room. She couldn't imagine violating someone else's privacy like that. No, she wasn't going to do it. Besides, it didn't seem like there was anything all that interesting to discover among the posters, maps, and trophies anyway.

Instead, she decided to reread Charlie's message, which for some reason she hadn't deleted. He had sent it through Facebook but was one of those people who used an icon instead of a real profile picture, so she had no idea what he looked like. She clicked on his page, but since they weren't officially "friends" as far as Facebook was concerned, she had limited access to his profile and could only find out the basic stuff like where he lived. But she could peruse his friend list and clicked "view all friends" to find out a little more about him. She didn't fully subscribe to the theory that your friends defined you, but she sat up a little straighter when she saw the literally dozens of cute girls on his list.

Now that she was starting to piece his life together, she had a sudden desire to know more. She was also starting to consider that she might have been wrong and that perhaps Charlie wasn't so boring after all. For all she knew, he was the bold, daring type and had already done a clean sweep of her room. She shuddered to think of what embarrassing thing she might have left behind for him to find, like a stray pair of underwear (the decidedly unsexy kind she bought at Rite Aid for $3.99) or one of the "goals" lists she sometimes made.

Maybe *she* was the dorky one.

She got on her hands and knees to peek under the bed. Large piles of mostly dirty clothes (the signs of a last-minute cleanup), random sports equipment, and a few dust bunnies covered the floor. She didn't know what she was hoping to find, but she was relieved not to stumble on anything X-rated.

She looked in the dresser next, expecting it to be empty, but it was crammed with T-shirts, boxer shorts, and various other items of clothing. Typical guy, she thought, leaving her nowhere to put her clothes. There was no way she was going to live out of a suitcase for the next two months, so she dumped his stuff out on the floor and then transferred it all to her empty bags once she had unpacked. Since she'd never had a boyfriend, there was something weirdly exciting about touching his clothes. She wasn't used to the way they felt, or how they smelled close up.

Celeste's voice echoed through her head as she noticed a drawer that ran flush with the desk, making it easy to miss. Any lingering guilt over invading his privacy subsided and was replaced with the thrill of finding out what was inside.

Molly sat back down and convinced herself that as a snooper she had the right, nay, the obligation, to open it.

She tucked her fingers beneath the drawer and pulled, but nothing happened. She tugged harder, thinking that it was probably so jammed with forgotten notes and mail and pens that something had gotten stuck in the back. But no matter how much she tried, it wouldn't budge. She looked closer and realized that it wasn't stuck at all.

It was locked.

How very, very interesting.

• • •

Before Charlie was awake enough to remember where he was, he felt the soft lavender sheets rubbing against his skin, wrapped around his body like a cocoon. He breathed in their smell, a blend of spring flowers and fresh air, like they'd been hung outside to dry.

He opened his eyes and adjusted to the brightness of the room, which was what had eventually woken him up. He'd left the window and curtain open so that the cat could come in, but it appeared that he'd taken off at some point after Charlie had fallen asleep. It had been kind of soothing drifting off to the sound of his meows.

The mattress was so comfortable it was hard to get up. He lay there for a few minutes, gazing at the collage of photos on the wall facing him. He still didn't know which one was Molly, since her Facebook picture featured three girls, a pretty blonde, an Indian girl, and another girl whose face was partially covered by her dark hair. The same three girls were plastered all over the corkboard.

He got up and walked over to get a closer look, pulling on a pair of sweatpants as he went. There were a few fashion magazine cutouts pinned up too, but they seemed long forgotten, buried beneath the photographs. Each of the girls seemed so different that if it hadn't been for the dozens of snapshots of them together, Charlie would never have pegged them as friends.

The blonde stood out most; not because there were more pictures of her than anyone else, but she was as close to objectively hot as anyone could get, with her long, wavy hair, tall, slim build, pronounced features, and smooth, tanned skin. She seemed to know it too, the way she mugged for the camera with her pouty lips and visible cleavage, like she just might get discovered in her own room. He figured she must be Molly, since she seemed like the type to assemble her own wall of fame.

The Indian girl was also pretty, but in a more subdued way, and the girl with dark hair seemed just as elusive up on the wall as she did in the profile picture, like she didn't want to be fully seen. In almost every picture she looked off to the side or wore sunglasses, which only added to her mystery.

"Charlieeeeee," Mia squealed, followed by the familiar rumbling of four galloping footsteps and the twins' thunderous entrance into his room. Mia, chased by Heather, stormed in first, crashing right into him.

"How many times do I have to tell you? You can't come in unless you knock first," he snapped on impact. "Out! Same rules apply in L.A."

"But you have a visitor!" Mia announced, barging in to inspect his room. "And we heard you, so you weren't even asleep."

"Right. And are you the visitor?" he asked, watching Heather follow her in.

"Actually, *I* am," a voice called out from the hall.

Charlie opened the door wider, startled to find the blonde from the collage standing in front of him.

"Oh, hey," he said awkwardly, wondering why Molly was there and not in Boulder. "Uh, can I . . . help you?"

"I'm Celeste," she said, extending her hand. "Your mom let me in and said I could come up. I live down the street and Molly forgot a couple of things."

"Oh," Charlie said, surprised that he had gotten it wrong. "I thought this was your room." Celeste looked at him, perplexed. "You're all over the wall of fame," he explained, pointing to exhibit A.

"Molly and I have been best friends since we were little," Celeste explained, marching into the room. "This is Molly," she said, pointing to the unassuming dark-haired girl, the last person to whom Charlie had thought the room, or, more specifically the collage, would have belonged.

Celeste surveyed the room with her hands on her hips and her chest jutting out of her miniature tank top.

Charlie could tell this girl was a handful from the photos alone, but her entrance confirmed it. There was no disputing that she was hot, though, even if her boobs did stand at attention like that, at right angles to the rest of her body.

Real or fake? he wondered. He was beginning to understand what Teddy meant.

"There you are!" Heather said to Celeste, pointing her out on the wall.

"And there too," Mia added. "And there, and everywhere. Are you a model or something?" she asked Celeste.

"Hardly," Celeste snorted. "But thanks, honey. You're sweet."

"What are you guys still doing here? Out!" Charlie said.

"But your room is better!" Heather protested. "We want to trade!"

"You two should come over to my house if you want to see a fabulous room," Celeste suggested. She glanced quickly at Charlie. "You should too."

"Thanks!" the girls said in unison as they ran out giggling.

"I'm sorry about that," Charlie said. "You don't need to entertain them."

"I don't mind," Celeste said. "They're cute."

"You say that now. . . . " Charlie warned. "So, what do you need?"

"Actually? Her sheets," Celeste explained.

"Her sheets," Charlie repeated, processing the request. "You know, we do have sheets in Boulder. It's not like we live in caves or anything," he said, even though he sometimes considered it.

"Hey, don't shoot the messenger," Celeste said, popping a piece of gum in her mouth. "I'm only fulfilling a request. And you haven't even told me your name."

"Charlie," he said.

"Mmm. It's so funny," she said. "You're sleeping in Moll's room, and she's sleeping in yours."

"She's in mine?" he asked. He didn't know why he felt surprised. No self-respecting person over the age of twelve would choose his sisters' room over his. Still, his room was so . . . well . . . *opposite* of Molly's.

"Indeed she is, Obi-Wan," Celeste said, winking at Charlie before walking into the closet.

Charlie felt the flush of red in his cheeks. The *Star Wars* sheets had been his favorite, a birthday gift from his moms when he was eight, but a combination of ten percent nostalgia and ninety percent laziness had led to their active use almost ten years later. He'd never thought about a stranger sleeping on them, or, worse, her hot best friend finding out about it.

Celeste reappeared dressed in a yellow-patterned dress and stood in front of the full-length mirror on the back of the closet door. "What do you think?" she asked. "Too yellow?"

It was definitely yellow, but that wasn't all he noticed. She twirled around in front of the mirror, causing the skirt to lift up, revealing a glimpse of lace panties underneath.

"Uh, weren't you looking for sheets?' he asked, unable to tell if she was hitting on him or if she just flirted with everyone.

"Oh, don't worry," she explained, gently punching his arm. "Molly always lets me in here. She gave me permission to borrow stuff all summer. But don't stress," she added, reading the expression on Charlie's face, "I won't, like, use my key or barge in without knocking or anything."

"Good to know," he said, hoping she would drop in again. "I prefer people who knock anyway."

"Is that so?" she said suggestively, brushing past him on her way toward the door. "So, Charlie, do you have any friends here?" she asked, flipping her hair over her shoulder.

"I think that remains to be seen," he responded.

"Well, if you're not too busy, I know of a cool party in the hills on Monday night. I'll pop by and get you. Eight P.M." Without waiting for a response, she walked back into the hall.

"Aren't you forgetting the sheets?" he called after her.

"Nope," she said, opening a hall closet and taking a pile with her before going back downstairs and out the front door.

From: Charlie
To: Molly
Date: June 15, 2008 11:11 A.M. PST
Subject: Sheets

Hey Molly,

Thanks for the tips. Cheese was gone by the time I woke up, but I'll try them out next time he appears (if he does, now that he knows you're gone).

In other news, your friend Celeste was just here to pick up your sheets. I guess that means you are staying in my room after all. Don't worry, I'm not taking the sheet retrieval mission personally and neither is Luke Skywalker.

Since we're on the topic of bed linens, what am I supposed to do with the pillows when I go to sleep? I slept on top of all seventy-two of them last night, but something tells me that's not what they're meant for.

Charlie

From: Molly
To: Charlie
Date: June 15, 2008 3:27 P.M. MST
Subject: Re: Sheets

I hope Celeste didn't barge in on you or anything embarrassing like that. She basically lives at my house, so she's not used to things like ringing the bell or knocking, especially when it comes to my room. Also, don't be alarmed if you see her walking off with clothes from my closet—she has permission (sort of).

No offense about the sheets, but you have to admit, mine are pretty awesome—hence the need for my emergency care package. It has absolutely nothing to do with your crush on Jar Jar Binks or anything. Seriously.

I usually stuff the pillows in the space between the night table and the wall, but good to know they serve a purpose besides looking pretty.

Molly

From: Charlie
To: Molly
Date: June 15, 2008 4:06 P.M. PST
Subject: Re:Re: Sheets

Celeste did disappear into your closet and came out wearing something else (something much nicer, I might add). Just let me know when you need me to start keeping tabs. With two younger sisters, I'm pretty good at being the heavy.

Also, I was wondering, what makes your sheets smell like they do? If I could think of a less creepy way of asking you that, believe me, I would. I also considered not asking, but you know, curiosity . . .

C

From: Molly
To: Charlie
Date: June 15, 2008 9:19 P.M. MST
Subject: Re:Re:Re: Sheets

My secret is Tide spring scent. . . . Here's another secret: there's a lifetime supply in the laundry room.
M.

Last night I had a dream about you / In this dream I'm dancing right beside you.

—Daft Punk, "Digital Love"

Molly hadn't been able to stop thinking about the desk drawer and what might be inside it. She wondered why it was locked—if Charlie had had some weird premonition that she was going to snoop, or if it was just his standard practice to maintain some semblance of privacy. He did have younger sisters, after all.

Everything about his room suggested he didn't have much of a personality—at least not one Molly would normally find interesting. But there was something compelling about his e-mails, his cute comments, and his confidence that she didn't expect. Molly wondered what Charlie thought of *her* so far—how she came off to a total stranger, what her room and her belongings said about who she was. She still had no idea what he looked like and hadn't been able to find a picture of him anywhere.

She stared again at the locked drawer. She had already scoured the room looking for the key, but with no luck. Charlie must have taken it with him.

Breaking into the desk was not an option. Not only would it be taking snooping to a whole new level, but Charlie would know she'd done it as soon as he returned. Celeste would probably have some convincing yet utterly ridiculous plan to cover it up, but Molly didn't even want to hear it. The drawer was going to have to remain locked for the summer. Even if the suspense killed her.

She was about to get up when the bling of an incoming IM distracted her. It was from Celeste.

Cshells: u there?

Mollypop: hey...where have u been?

Cshells: two words: sale and barneys.

Mollypop: ok, ok. and? what was he like?

Cshells: someone's very curious.

Mollypop: you'd be too if someone was living in your room.

Cshells: please . . . i'm used to strangers in my bed. . . . lol!

Mollypop: i'm rolling my eyes right now. so, did you get my sheets?

Molly already knew the answer, of course, but she wasn't ready to tell Celeste about her e-mails with Charlie. Not yet anyway.

Cshells: of course. i'm a good little messenger. and the boy is nothing special. his name's charlie or something.

Molly felt a sinking sense of disappointment. It was stupid, but she'd been hoping that Charlie was hot. If nothing else, at least she'd know that there was a cute boy out there in the world who liked her enough to write her e-mails.

Mollypop: really? then what's he like?

Cshells: your room looks the same btw. did you snoop like a good girl???

Molly paused. How much should she say?

Cshells: hello? u still there?

Mollypop: i'm here. . . . yup i looked. . . . didn't find anything exciting, tho.

Cshells: well, that's not surprising. . . . he's not the living-on-the-edge type. your sheets should get there by tomorrow, fyi.

Mollypop: thx so much. totally owe you.

Cshells: gotta go. my cousin's taking me to some fabulous pool party. TTYL and i expect a FULL report on the boulder mountain men. keep digging! xo

Mollypop: ok . . . don't hold your breath. xxx

It was official. Celeste would laugh if she knew that Molly had actually taken Charlie's e-mails seriously. It was time to squash whatever silly notions she might have had about Charlie Richards.

• • •

From: Charlie
To: Molly
Date: June 16, 2008 10:26 A.M. PST
Subject: Catless

Hey Molly,

I know that Cheese isn't technically your cat, but he hasn't been around since that first time and I was wondering if I should be worried and alert the lost cat authorities. Maybe he's in a funk or something without you around. Should I hang some string cheese out the window so that he doesn't starve?

Also, how's Boulder so far?

Charlie

From: Molly
To: Charlie
Date: June 16, 2008 4:49 P.M. MST
Subject: Re: Catless

Hi Charlie,

Don't worry about Cheese. I guarantee he'll be back, especially once he realizes there's still a steady supply of food. Then he'll never leave you alone.

It's really beautiful here (I've never seen such high mountains), but I haven't really done much yet. I went to the Pearl Street Mall the other day, where I somehow found myself filling out a job application—don't even ask! What have you been up to so far?

Molly

From: Charlie
To: Molly
Date: June 16, 2008 11:42 P.M. PST
Subject: Re:Re: Catless

M,

Can I call you M? or Em? While we're on the topic, do you have a nickname? I don't. It's just Charlie, and it's not short for Charles, but it's amazing how many people just assume it is and call me that. Anyway, the best way to see Boulder is on a bike, so if you didn't bring one, feel free to borrow one of mine from the garage. If you're just staying on-road, use the red one near the door. You can adjust the seat by turning the knob beneath it, and there's a basket of helmets under the bench at the back. If you're up for trail riding let me know—I can tell you where to go. Speaking of trails, I just discovered Griffith Park. Pretty awesome.

So what's this job you applied for? I know you said don't ask, but now I'm curious, so you have to tell me.

By the way, what's up with all the sketches and the sewing machine? Are you a famous designer I should know about?

Charlie

P.S. Cheese just appeared in the window. Glad I didn't scare him away.

From: Molly
To: Charlie
Date: June 17, 2008 8:16 A.M. MST
Subject: terra firma

See? I told you he'd be back. Now you have a little gray friend for life—that's the thing about cats—once they know your scent they'll never forget you. If my mom weren't allergic, I'd probably have a million. I'm not a crazy-cat-lady-in-training or anything weird like that.... I just feel so bad for strays.

I'm not a nickname person either. Only three people are allowed to call me Molls, but that's just because they've known me forever. That said, you can call me M if I can call you C. They seem fitting for people who don't like nicknames.

I'm not exactly the athletic type, and the last bike I was on had three wheels, so I'm probably better off with both feet on the ground. I'm sure I'm missing out, but at least I'd be sparing any pedestrians out there I'd crash into. This probably sounds ridiculous, since you're clearly a bike expert, so don't think any less of me!

Oh—and I'm not a famous designer but it's sweet of you to put it like that. I hope that one day I will be (a designer, that is), but that's a long way off from now.... I still have a lot to learn.

I just got a call about the job and I got it! So not what I was planning, but I was kind of caught off guard. So, in about an hour I'll officially be an employee at Second Time Around.... It's a thrift store on the Pearl

Street Mall that I'm sure no one's ever heard of. . . . I kind of have a thing for vintage, so hopefully it'll be fun. . . . Okay, I feel like I'm rambling, and I'm gonna be late, so I better go. . . . Have a great day, C!

M

"Can you love a player?"

— Viola de Lesseps, *Shakespeare in Love*

"Where does this one go?" Molly asked, taking a men's burgundy velvet vest with a ton of potential from a cardboard box.

Penelope peered over the reading glasses perched on her nose to get a better look. "Front right corner, honey. Put it with the blazers. That's the first vest I've seen in years."

Molly shook it out and smoothed her hands over the fabric, imagining the various outfits she could pair it with—after making the necessary additions and adjustments, of course. When Molly left the store two days before, working there, let alone ever coming back, was the last thing she thought would ever happen. But when Penelope called with the offer, Molly accepted. She had spent the better part of the interim days in the house while her mother and Ron went off on local excursions. They had invited her along, but she had continuously turned them down in the name of working on her Cynthia Vincent application. While she had officially given up on completing it, it provided the perfect excuse to avoid hanging out with the "lovebirds."

And if she was honest, she'd have to admit that she was secretly holding out hope that a brilliant idea would come knocking—one that would easily win her the internship.

But no amount of staring at a blank page, perusing fashion websites, or checking her e-mail inspired her or made the time alone pass any faster. The job at the thrift store had gone from no-way-in-hell to might-as-well in less than forty-eight hours. Sifting through old clothes for a few hours a day gave Molly a reason to get out of the house, and if it didn't work out, she could always quit. Rina was a firm believer that every open door was a potential opportunity for life change, and Molly wasn't in a position to be turning any down.

"You're making good progress," Penelope observed. Molly had already unpacked and sorted through three boxes. "It's amazing what an extra pair of hands will do. Let's see what else I have in back."

Penelope led Molly through a door behind the desk into another room. Maybe it was that she'd been in a rush to leave the last time she was there, but Molly was only now noticing that Penelope had style. "I like your outfit," she said, taking in her white tunic paired with a silk turquoise scarf draped loosely around her neck.

"Thanks, honey," Penelope said, smoothing her blouse. "Where is that damn thing?" she grumbled, feeling along the wall with her other hand. "Ah, there it is."

The room lit up, revealing overflowing shelves displaying old costume jewelry, intricate boxes, and every kind of knickknack you'd find at a flea market. More racks of clothes stood against the back wall, and three naked mannequins, one of which was missing an arm, were crammed into a corner.

"Wow," Molly said, walking in. "There's so much stuff in here."

"Junk. All junk, but I have a hard time throwing anything out. Not much to sell back here except what's in this pile," Penelope said, pointing to a box by her feet.

Molly was already on the other side of the room, inspecting the mannequins. "Why don't you use these?"

"You know, I picked those up at a garage sale a couple years back and forgot they were even here. Pretty silly, since they're staring me right in the face."

"Don't take this the wrong way," Molly started, "but I think a display could be good for business. I don't mind making one for you." Molly loved window displays, especially ones that took risks and paired unusual items together to create a new look or a variation on a style. Molly also believed that as a designer it was key to know not only how to make clothes but how to put them together, and she'd always wanted to create a window display.

"Darling, do I mind?" Penelope said. "That's the best offer I've gotten all year! Let me dust these off and help you bring them out front."

They carried the mannequins one at a time through the store and stood them side by side in the display. Penelope wiped down the window while Molly spent the next hour carefully scouring the racks for clothes to dress them in.

Once she narrowed it down to a few select items, Penelope brought her a box of pins and Molly got to work. Dozens of people streamed by, all of whom seemed to turn and stare at Molly standing up there, like she was on display too. Once she got going, though, she became so absorbed in mixing and matching outfits that she forgot about the eyes on her—until there was a knock at the window. Molly didn't hear it until it came a second time, louder and more deliberate. She turned around with three pins clenched between her teeth and saw Sylvia, the red-haired girl from the coffee shop, standing out on the sidewalk, with a confused look on her face.

Molly stuck the pins in the back of a men's pin-striped shirt that one of the mannequins was wearing to give it more shape, then hopped down off the mounted pedestal. "I'll be out front," she called out to Penelope, who was sorting through paperwork at her desk.

"It's about time you had a break. Take your time, honey."

"Wow," Sylvia said, when Molly came out. "Who knew there was anything that cool in there."

"That's why I thought a display might help. It's obviously not finished yet."

"But it looks amazing already! I've lived here my whole life and never even been in this store. It always seemed so old and creepy, but now I want that outfit," she said, pointing to the mannequin in gray-colored cords, the velvet burgundy vest, and a delicate white blouse, creating a Ralph Lauren circa 1982 effect; the other two were still in a state of semi-undress, but Molly had at least masked the missing arm with a hand-knit poncho she had dug up in the back.

"You should come in and see what else we have," Molly said, ignoring Sylvia's comment about the store. She had felt the same way the first time she'd stood in front of the window, but now that she was an official employee, her perspective had started to change, and she even felt a tiny bit defensive about the shop.

"So you work here now?" Sylvia asked.

"Yup, as of this morning."

"Okay, you're definitely not the usual summer tourist," Sylvia said. "So why *are* you here? I take it it wasn't because of this job. There must be a million better thrift stores in L.A."

"I didn't have much say in the matter," Molly explained. Off Sylvia's look, she added, "My mom and her new husband decided it would be great if I tagged along on their extremely long honeymoon."

"Romantic." Sylvia laughed. "So where are you newlyweds staying?"

"Very funny," Molly said, rolling her eyes. It was nice to have someone her own age to talk to. "We're doing a house swap with a family around here. We're staying in their house, they're staying in ours. Now that's romance."

"I've heard about that kind of thing," Sylvia said. "A bunch of people around here do it. I'd kill to escape my life right now if it were a remote possibility."

"It's not all it's cracked up to be, trust me."

Sylvia's eyes welled up and she sat down on a nearby park bench.

Molly felt her stomach twist. Had she said the wrong thing? She followed Sylvia and sat down next to her—watched her wringing her hands, heard her ragged breathing.

It was heartache, no doubt about it. Molly was familiar with the feeling. "You don't have to talk about it if you don't want to."

"No. No, it's okay," Sylvia said, dabbing her eyes with a tissue to stop her mascara from running. "It's just that my boyfriend and I broke up, and I guess I'm still having a hard time facing reality."

"I understand," Molly said. She didn't, technically, since she'd never had a boyfriend, but if she had, she wouldn't want it to end either.

"I totally fell for him. My friends warned me that he was a player, but

I refused to listen. I thought things were different with me, that he really cared." She blew her nose. "I was so wrong."

"What happened?" Molly asked tentatively, not wanting to pry too much.

"He came over after school one day and announced that it was over. Just like that, completely out of the blue."

"Did he say why?"

Molly's question brought on another round of tears. "Because he didn't like me anymore."

"Wow. I can't believe he said that." She was amazed that anyone could be so heartless. "What a jerk."

"I know," Sylvia agreed. "I was such an idiot."

"You can't blame yourself. He's the one who has the problem, and you deserve a lot more than that."

"Thanks," Sylvia said, managing a half-smile. For a moment, they sat in comfortable silence.

"Why don't you come in and try it on?" Molly suggested, nodding toward the mannequin's outfit.

"My break's over," Sylvia said. "I better get back." She rose from her seat, then paused. "Thanks for listening, though."

"Sure," Molly said. "Anytime."

• • •

The house was empty when Charlie returned. Sally and Lisa were still at work, and the girls were god knows where with Celeste, who had come by that morning and offered to take them on an excursion. She had invited Charlie too, but he'd opted to spend the day alone. There was only so much girl talk he could take, and he was going to that party with Celeste in a few hours anyway.

He went up to his room, kicked off his muddy shoes, and left them by the door. Three days in and he'd managed to avoid ruining anything yet. He turned on the stereo and played his current favorite song, "Together," by the Raconteurs. He took off his shirt, sweaty from his ride, a worn red vintage tee from Second Time Around advertising Coke, and lay down on the bed with his laptop. Cheese suddenly appeared and jumped up on his lap.

"Hey, guy," he said, rubbing the cat's chin. "Let's see what news Molly brings from Boulder." He opened his laptop and checked his inbox, which was empty. "Out of luck, Cheese-man. She's probably still hard at work— unlike you and me."

He got up and walked over to the wall of photos and stared at the ones of Molly. "So who else calls her Molls?" he asked, looking down at his feet, where the cat was doing figure eights between his legs. "Is it her boyfriend, little guy? Is that what you're trying to tell me?"

"Um, excuse me, I don't mean to interrupt your little moment, but we're going to be late." Celeste was standing in the doorway, her arms loaded with shopping bags.

"Whoa! How long have you been standing there?" Charlie asked, hoisting the cat up in his arms to cover himself.

"Long enough to know that you're not ready . . . and that you talk to cats. Out loud."

"Where are my sisters?" Charlie asked, changing the subject. He grabbed the nearest shirt, which happened to be the one he'd just taken off, and put it back on inside out.

"They're in their room, trying on their new purchases. Expect a fashion show in about five," she said, coming into the room. "And I see that

someone's shy," she said, tugging on his sleeve. "Ewww. And way sweaty."
She jerked her hand away.

"That's what happens when you exert yourself," he said, picking a towel
up off the floor. "I was mountain biking for the past three hours."

"Oh, believe me, I know how to exert myself, just not on a bike," she said.

"Do guys really fall for that kind of line out here?"

"I think you know the answer to that," Celeste said, dropping her purse
and all the bags on the floor and disappearing into the closet.

"So how much money, exactly, did my sisters spend on your little
adventure?" he called out.

"So uptight," she scolded playfully, reappearing in a short black dress
with a plunging vee that got lost in her cleavage. It was sexy, but definitely
a size too small. "It was my treat." She rotated back and forth in front of
the mirror a few times and darted back into the closet. "You can put your
eyeballs back in their sockets now."

"Was I that obvious?" he asked, with a sly grin. He wasn't used to girls
being this forward. They usually made their affections known in more
subtle, nonverbal ways, like sitting next to him at lunch or in class.

"Men always are. Boys especially." She came back out in a white sundress
with lace stitching. It was beautiful. He wondered if Molly had made it, if
she had made everything hanging in the closet.

"Didn't you just go shopping?" Charlie asked, gesturing toward the bags
from Kitson, Barneys, and Saks on the carpet. Molly wasn't kidding when
she warned that Celeste would be raiding her closet.

"Are you trying to tell me this doesn't look good?"

He just looked at her. Now she was fishing for a compliment—they both
knew she looked amazing.

"I'll take that as a yes," she said, prancing out of the room, taking her bags with her. "Now go shower. The party started at five. We're late."

"You said eight," Charlie called out after her.

He switched his shirt for a clean one from the pile on the floor—the dumped contents of his duffel bag—and slid on a pair of jeans. In lieu of a shower, he ran his hands through his hair, matted from the bike helmet, and sat down at the desk. He opened his laptop and began a new e-mail to Molly.

To: Molly
From: Charlie
Date: June 17, 2008 5:55 P.M. PST
Subject: Congrats

Hey M,

Cheese and I are sitting here wondering how your first day went. Not only have I heard of Second Time Around but I've been there many times. True story. Where else could I get T-shirts with slogans from the seventies? Tell Penelope I say hello.

We're also wondering which three people get to call you Molls. Or I'm wondering anyway. I'm guessing that two of them are all over that wall of fame of yours (Celeste and the other girl?) but who's the third?

And you definitely do not have to be an athlete to ride a bike, or an expert, or even experienced. Trust me. It's now my goal to get you on one by the end of the summer.

C

"You're still not ready?" Celeste accused, reappearing with a face full of makeup.

"You have to chill out," Charlie said, hitting send and quickly snapping his laptop shut before she had a chance to read the screen.

"Ooh, secrets," she taunted, peering over his shoulder.

Charlie ignored her. "All right, let's go," he said, leading the way to the door.

• • •

The mountains seemed to follow Molly no matter which way she turned. The farthermost peak was capped with snow and served as a beacon to point her in the right direction home. She couldn't remember the last time she had walked anywhere other than across the street to Celeste's. In L.A., it just wasn't done. But it felt good to breathe in the fresh, clean air, and to be free like that.

She had made it through her first day of work. It had been a good first day and she was beginning to feel like she could do this. She could make it through the summer.

"Hey! Molly?" a girl's voice called out. "Is that you?"

Molly turned around and saw Sylvia biking toward her, her red hair flowing loose behind her like a cape. She glided to a stop and pulled her bike up on the curb. "Where you going?"

"Home," Molly said. It wasn't really home, but she didn't know how else to describe it. "We're staying in Boulder Canyon."

"That's where I live," Sylvia said. "You want a ride?"

"Um, no, that's okay," Molly declined, trying to figure out how that could possibly work. "I'm not very good on bikes."

"It's easy, I'll show you." Sylvia stood up and steadied the bike by holding the handlebars. "If you sit sideways here," she said, motioning to the flat rack behind her seat, "you can hold on to me and I'll do all the work."

"Okay," Molly capitulated. She hoisted herself onto the rack and wrapped her arms around Sylvia's waist. "Tell me if I squeeze too hard."

"Don't worry. Just sit back and enjoy the ride."

As the bike started moving, Molly thought she was going to slide off and pull Sylvia down with her. Once she got used to the bumpy rhythm, she relaxed enough to loosen her grip around Sylvia's waist and enjoy the breeze whipping past her. Molly might not have been the one technically riding the bike, but she was at least sitting on one, which was a step in the right direction. She couldn't wait to tell Charlie. It was strange that after knowing him for only two days, there was already something that she only wanted to share with him.

"Which way?" Sylvia asked as they approached an intersection.

Molly looked up at the mountains. "Left here and then it's your third right."

"Where now?" Sylvia asked, turning onto Molly's street.

"Keep going a little farther," Molly instructed. "Okay, slow down . . . and stop . . . here," she said, sliding off the rack and hopping up onto the sidewalk in front of the house.

"*This* is where you're staying?" Sylvia asked, still straddling the bike.

"Yeah, you want to come in?"

"Um, sure," Sylvia said, slowly getting off the bike and walking it up the driveway and leaning it against the side of the house. She hesitated by the entrance.

"Come in!" Molly said, holding the front door open for her. "Don't worry, nobody's home."

Sylvia came in and Molly led the way upstairs. When she turned on the lights in her room, Sylvia gasped and retreated into the hallway.

"Hey! Are you okay?" Molly asked. "You look really pale."

"I'm sorry," Sylvia said. "This is just . . . I can't be here."

"What is it?" Molly asked, trying to decipher what had just happened. "I don't understand."

"This house . . . that room," Sylvia muttered, backing away. "It's Charlie's."

Molly felt a smile spread across her face. "Yes, it is! Do you two know each other?" Her brain suddenly flooded with questions. She wanted to ask, *How tall is he? What's his favorite song? Is he really as good on his bike as he says?*

Sylvia swallowed noisily, a strangled sob. "Charlie Richards is my ex-boyfriend."

Molly reeled. Sylvia's boyfriend, the total jerk, was Charlie? *Her* Charlie?

Sylvia ran down the stairs and out the door. "I'm so sorry," Molly whispered as she watched her go.

• • •

When Molly came back to the room she went straight for her laptop. She had been waiting to check her e-mail all day, hoping to hear from Charlie. But now that there was a new message from him in her inbox, she felt sick to her stomach. As much as she wanted to believe that he was genuinely interested in her, that a guy like him *could* be interested in her, now she had every reason not to. The whole situation was better left alone. If not, there was one thing she could count on—getting hurt. Guys like Charlie were all the same.

Molly opened his e-mail. When she finished reading it, instead of clicking on the reply button, she hit delete.

If you do not tell the truth about yourself, you cannot tell it about other people.

—Virginia Woolf

Celeste's BMW SUV pulled up behind a line of other BMWs, Audis, and Mercedes idling at a valet stand. "I thought you said this was a barbecue," Charlie remarked, as two men in red vests appeared on either side of the car and opened their doors. The man on the driver's side handed Celeste a ticket in exchange for her keys.

"It is." She locked arms with Charlie and walked toward the fifteen-foot gate enclosing the house. "Welcome to Hollywood."

A man in a black suit emerged from the guardhouse to the left with a pen and a clipboard. Celeste met him halfway and spent the next five minutes convincing him that she was "on the list." She was the most presumptuous person Charlie had ever met, but she was effective. He had to give her that. In moments, the gate opened and they walked through.

"Good friend of yours?" Charlie teased.

"Technicalities." Celeste shrugged. "Just follow me."

"Wow," Charlie said, as a football-field–size lawn spread out before them. The grass gradually sloped up to a whitewashed Spanish hacienda with a red-tiled roof.

This wasn't just any house, he thought. It was an honest-to-goodness mansion.

"This way." Celeste led Charlie up the grassy hill and around the side of the house. A DJ stood behind a table, blasting hip-hop remixes while at least a hundred people congregated around the pool and the garden beyond.

"So what do you think?" Celeste asked, scanning the crowd. A waitress in a skimpy miniskirt darted past, balancing a tray of tequila shots above her head.

"Very intimate," Charlie said with a smirk. "Just what comes to mind when I think 'summer barbecue among friends.'"

"So is that what you do in Boulder?" Celeste asked. "Try to impress the girls with sarcasm?"

"You nailed it. That's me." He paused. "How's it working out so far?"

"I'll let you know after I have a drink." She took off toward the outdoor bar by the pool.

Charlie watched her go.

"Aren't you coming?"

He started toward her just as some guy she seemed to know swept her onto the dance floor. She jumped right into the beat, shimmying her body against his, with her eyes locked on Charlie the whole time. There was no denying it was kind of hot.

When the song was over, she kissed the guy on the cheek and headed back toward Charlie, silently brushing past him as she continued on to the bar. Within thirty seconds she was flirting with some other guy at the front of the line, trying to convince him to let her cut in. She caught Charlie's eye and motioned for him to join her, but something was holding him back.

"I'll be over here," he called out.

He wandered off along the perimeter of the garden toward a large empty patio on the other side of the house. The deck extended twenty feet beyond the grass, giving him the feeling that he was floating over the canyon below. He stood watching as the sun disappeared behind the peak on the other side of the canyon, spotting the sky pink over the brightening city lights.

Celeste was probably wondering where he'd gone, but he didn't care. For some reason, all he could think about was Molly.

• • •

To: Molly
From: Charlie
Date: June 18, 2008 12:13 A.M. PST
Subject: stuff

_____

Hey M,

Are you awake? Celeste took me to some fancy party in the Hollywood Hills and I just got home. It had a valet, bartenders, a doorman with a clipboard . . . WOW. Are all L.A. parties like that? It was definitely different. The barbecues I usually go to consist of some dogs and a few six-packs in someone's backyard. Not too exciting, but it works.

Anyway, I'll be up for a while if you get this.

C

To: Molly
From: Charlie
Date: June 20, 2008 2:57 P.M. PST
Subject: hello

Hey Molly,

Just checking in to say hi. I'm sure you're really busy with your new job but I also wanted to make sure everything's okay, since I haven't heard back from you in a while.

Charlie

To: Charlie
From: Molly
Date: June 21, 2008 8:50 A.M. MST
Subject: Re: hello

Dear Charlie,

Sorry I haven't gotten back to you. I have been really busy at the store. Also, I've been getting to know your ex-girlfriend Sylvia. I hope you're enjoying L.A.

Molly

To: Molly
From: Charlie
Date: June 21, 2008 9:15 A.M. PST
Subject: Re: Re: hello

Yikes!

Listen, Molly, I don't know what Sylvia's been saying about me, but I can imagine it's not great. We dated for a couple of months and broke up a couple weeks ago. I know I didn't handle things well, and I'm not proud of it. I don't want to get in the way if you guys are becoming friends, but at least give me a chance to explain my side of things. I hope you write back.

Charlie

To: Charlie
From: Molly
Date: June 21, 2008 5:52 P.M. MST
Subject: okay . . .

I'm listening. —M

To: Molly
From: Charlie
Date: June 21, 2008 6:01 P.M. PST
Subject: Re: okay . . .

Sylvia and I started hanging out in the spring, and before I knew it we were dating. I've never really admitted this to anyone, but I started to lose interest in her after the first few weeks. I guess I was hoping that if we got to know each other better, there'd be more of a connection, but nothing ever changed and I could never confide in her about anything or even have a conversation like this. So when I found out we were going to L.A., it seemed like a good way to end things without hurting her feelings. That kind of backfired, though, because she didn't understand why we couldn't keep dating when I was going to be back in two months. Things kinda went downhill from there, and she wouldn't let me leave until I told her if I still had feelings for her. At that point, I just told her the truth.

Anyway, that's my full disclosure. I hope you don't dismiss me as some typical jerk. I'm really not, and for some reason it's important to me that you know that.

Charlie

To: Charlie
From: Molly
Date: June 21, 2008 10:58 P.M. MST
Subject: for the record . . .

I don't think you're a jerk

JULY

9

Only Connect.

—E.M. Forster, *Howards End*

Snowpeak99: u there?

Snowpeak99: it's me...charlie

Mollypop: i am! hi!

Snowpeak99: i got your IM address from facebook and noticed you were online so . . .

Mollypop: well, i'm really glad you noticed!

Snowpeak99: and i'm glad you're still awake.

Mollypop: yeah . . . i can be a bit of a night owl sometimes.

Snowpeak99: whoa . . . cheese just appeared. he must have cosmically sensed you or something.

Mollypop: that, or he knows there's food in his future. . . .

Snowpeak99: how's work been going?

Mollypop: pretty great so far . . . but i could spend hours sifting through old interesting clothes. . . .

Snowpeak99: what do you like about it?

Mollypop: i don't know. . . . i guess how you can take something that someone else has gotten rid of and turn it into something completely new and different.

Mollypop: i have all these ideas of how to make them more modern and stuff.

Snowpeak99: you should. i'm sure they'd look even better with your touch.

Mollypop: yeah, i don't think penelope hired me to take a scissors to her inventory.

Snowpeak99: she probably doesn't know what she's missing.

Snowpeak99: btw, do you have a boyfriend?

Mollypop: i'll let you know if i ever get inspired and convert a men's suit into a dress or something crazy like that . . . which might happen if I don't get to sleep. it's almost 2 a.m. here!!!!

Snowpeak99: sleep well

Snowpeak99: i'm fully aware that you completely ignored my question.

Mollypop: don't forget to feed cheese!!

Mollypop: and . . . no . . . I don't have a boyfriend.

Snowpeak99: glad to hear it.

Mollypop: good night, charlie.

Snowpeak99: good night, molly.

• • •

Molly lugged a full-length mirror from the pink room down the hall and propped it up against the wall in Charlie's room. Only a boy could survive without a mirror.

"That's better," she said to herself, adjusting the bright yellow sash she'd tied around her waist to cinch in the dress. It had looked more like a blue smock when she had found it buried deep on one of the racks at the store, but the addition of a simple piece of fabric she had repurposed from a torn silk blouse made all the difference.

She had been wearing at least one item from the store to work every day. In addition to the mannequins, it was the best form of advertising when people walked through the door. Molly thought of it as her own personal *Project Runway*–type challenge to try to come up with a cute outfit on a daily basis.

Looking at her reflection, she noticed a box on top of the bookcase behind her, pushed back against the wall. She hadn't seen it before. She pushed the desk chair against the bookcase, stepped up, and reached around until she felt the cardboard edges in her grasp. She pulled the box down, placed it on the floor, and sat cross-legged in front of it, contemplating what to do. It was an old Nike shoe box, which had clearly been stowed out of sight for a reason. Then again, if there were anything in it that was that personal, Molly imagined Charlie would have locked it away with his other secrets. Since this box wasn't sealed or taped shut, she removed the top and peered inside. No transgression committed. There were just a bunch of receipts and concert ticket stubs . . . and underneath, a small, old-fashioned gold key, the kind that might open a locked desk drawer.

Molly pulled it out and held it in the open palm of her hand. It was long and thin and had a certain weightiness, like it was meant for something special. She looked back at the drawer, thinking it could do no harm to test it. She went to the desk, slid the key into the lock as far as it would go, and turned it to the right twice until she heard something click.

It was unlocked.

Molly wanted so badly to pull the drawer open, to see what it was that Charlie held so dear that he had to lock away and hide the key. She wanted to know more about him, especially the parts that he normally kept to himself. But she couldn't bring herself to do it. She couldn't cross that line.

She turned the key to the left twice until it clicked, removed it from the lock, and put it back in the shoe box underneath the receipts. She stepped back up on the chair and tipped the box back onto the top shelf where she'd found it.

Her mom and Ron were already gone by the time she came down for breakfast. There was a note saying they'd driven out to Rocky National Park and would be back by dinner. The mornings were starting to be the only time she really saw her mom, for a meal, at least. Most nights Molly made her own dinner when she came home from work and ate alone while Laura and Ron were still out on some excursion. She preferred it this way, and her mom didn't press the issue.

She looked up at the clock and realized she was running late and didn't have time for breakfast. With no one to keep her company during the meal, she wasn't all that hungry anyway.

As she walked out the front door, a bike whizzed past. It would be so much faster that way, she thought, facing the twenty-minute walk ahead in the already blazing sun.

She turned around, went back in the house and through the side door into the garage. She had gone in a few times since she and Charlie had started to become friends. She liked the way the bikes looked all lined up like that, in order, clean, organized. It was like seeing another part of Charlie close up.

She scanned the wall for the red one and reached up to lift it off the wall. It wasn't as heavy as she'd been expecting, she thought, as she wheeled it out onto the driveway.

She hoisted her leg over the bar and could only reach the seat by standing on the tips of her toes. Remembering what Charlie had told her about the knob under the seat, she turned it to the right and, like he'd said, it lowered easily. She got back on, gripped the handlebars, and pushed off on the pedals. Thankfully, her dress was short enough to allow her to easily straddle the bar, and long enough to avoid flashing the city of Boulder on her way.

Molly was wobbly at first, but luckily there weren't enough people out on the street for her to be publicly shamed. As she struggled to get her rhythm, she cursed the person who'd come up with the expression "It's just like riding a bike." When she made it to the end of the block, she realized she had left in such a hurry that she'd forgotten to grab a helmet, but now that she was moving with a degree of momentum, she couldn't go back.

She turned left and pedaled fast for a few seconds to get up enough speed to coast for a while. Feeling more stable, she relaxed enough to enjoy the wind blowing her hair off her face. She wondered if Charlie felt the same way when he rode down these streets.

• • •

"I'm sorry I'm late," Molly called out, as she wheeled the bike through the store to the back room, where she placed it next to Penelope's.

"You know how I feel," Penelope said, getting up from the desk.

"Yes, I know," Molly said, rolling her eyes. "You think I work too much."

"I have to practically force you out that door every day just to make sure you get some sunshine on your face." She reached over and patted Molly's cheeks. Her hand felt soothing.

"You're forgetting I live in L.A., where it's sunny three hundred and sixty-two days a year. I'm not here for the weather."

Molly got to work pulling select pieces out from the back racks and hanging them more prominently in front. She had noticed after the first couple of days that most people came in looking for the same type of clothing on display in the window. If they didn't find it on the first rack or two, they never made it further.

"I feel so guilty keeping you stuck in here all day," Penelope said.

"You've only known me for a little more than two weeks, so you're not allowed to feel guilty yet." The job was no longer just an excuse to stay away from her mom and Ron. Molly now looked forward to coming in every day and often hung around long after her shift, talking to Penelope. "What do you think of these?" She held up a short black DKNY dress from the late eighties that was now back in style, and a simple oversize white blouse she'd paired with a wide brass-and-leather belt.

"Fabulous. You have the most exquisite taste. I honestly don't know what I did before you came along."

Molly blushed. "You chose everything in here. I'm just providing a different point of view."

"Your point of view has increased sales by almost fifteen percent in the past week. I updated the books this morning."

Penelope was obviously running a business, but Molly had never thought about the nuts and bolts that went into it, like pricing items and keeping sales records. It didn't even feel like a job since all she did all day was mix and match outfits. She did that at home exploring her own closet. The only difference was that now it was on a much bigger scale—with more eclectic and varied possibilities. "If that's actually true, then you shouldn't be telling me to work less, should you?"

Penelope shook her head and laughed.

Once Molly finished arranging the inventory, she sat down at the desk. She had lost track of time until the front door jingled. She looked down at a piece of paper with dress sketches all over it—she wasn't even aware that she had been drawing—and pushed it aside before getting up. "I've got it," she said to Penelope, who popped her head out from the back room.

When she approached the front, she saw it was Sylvia standing there. Molly hadn't seen her since that afternoon at the house.

"Hi." Sylvia waved. "Can I talk to you for a second?" She was wearing an oversize blouse, cinched at the waist with a men's striped tie over a denim miniskirt. It was virtually identical to one of the outfits Molly had put together for the window display.

"Yeah, of course," Molly said. She followed her outside to the park bench, motioning to Penelope, who was now at the desk, that she'd be right back.

"I'm really sorry about how I behaved last time I saw you," Sylvia began once they were seated. "I wanted to come by sooner, but I've honestly been way too embarrassed."

"You have nothing to apologize for or be ashamed of," Molly quickly jumped in. "It was an entirely surprising turn of events for both of us."

Sylvia sat forward. "So you *do* know Charlie?"

"No . . . we've never met. Ron—that's my stepfather—knows one of his moms." It was true, they had never met, only it didn't truthfully answer Sylvia's question. "I just mean, it was weird and you had every reason to be a little freaked out."

"I know, what are the chances, right?" Sylvia leaned back against the bench facing the window display. "I definitely wasn't expecting to see that room again." She laughed. "I won't miss those stupid sports posters or, oh

God, the *Star Wars* sheets. Don't tell me you have to sleep on them."

"No, I've never seen them." Molly didn't mean to lie again. It just came out. She kept waiting for Sylvia to acknowledge that she was wearing the same outfit as the mannequin in the window staring back at them, but she didn't say a word about it. Molly knew that as a designer she would have to get used to that kind of thing and even take it as a compliment, but somehow it didn't feel so flattering and made her feel resentful.

With the discovery of Sylvia and Charlie's past, Molly had initially thought she wasn't going to be able to be friends with Charlie. But now, it appeared that Sylvia was the one she'd have to let go.

"I better get back," Sylvia said, looking at her watch.

"Totally." Molly got up and walked with her to the door.

Sylvia turned to face her. "I know you said you don't know Charlie, but if you ever meet, can you, like, not tell him about any of this?"

"Of course," Molly agreed, lying to Sylvia a third time. "I won't say a word."

• • •

To: Charlie
From: Molly
Date: July 2, 2008 5:10 P.M. MST
Subject: news

Charlie. I have some news. I rode a bike today. Yes, you read correctly. I got over my ridiculous fear (inspired by being late) and rode your red bike to work. I may not have been that graceful, but I didn't crash or fall or cause any accidents (that I'm aware of). It felt completely amazing!! I even rode around the neighborhood for a while on my way home. . . . I'm going to bike to work again tomorrow. It's so much faster!!

The other headline is that I sketched for the first time today in weeks. Sketching for me is like writing in a journal for other people. It's the only thing that makes me feel calm and inspired. . . . It's kind of like an escape. I've never told anyone that before, but for some reason I felt like telling you. . . .

I'll be home later tonight if you want to IM. . . .

Molls

To: Molly
From: Charlie
Date: July 2, 2008 3:15 P.M. PST
Subject: Re: news

Congratulations! That's awesome! See? I knew you could do it. I also know what you mean about sketching, only for me it's riding my bike up in the mountains. I just crank my iPod and explore the trails for hours. It's this constant reminder that I can escape whenever I want to and also that there's so much more out there in the world, so much that's bigger than me. It's kind of humbling in a way. Now that you're on two wheels maybe you can see what I mean one day.

I'm off to explore the hills of L.A.

See you online at ten your time unless I hear from you.

C

Look at the stars / Look how they shine for you / And all the things you do.

—Coldplay, "Yellow"

As he approached the incline, Charlie switched to the highest gear and pumped his legs so hard he lifted off the seat. Cresting the top of the hill, the view unfolded on each side of the road, Los Angeles to the south and the San Fernando Valley to the north. He had heard of the infamous Mulholland Drive in songs and movies, but now he was experiencing it for himself, firsthand.

He'd eventually found his way up there through trial and error and was now heading west toward the ocean, curious how far the road would take him. He could have easily looked it up on Google maps, but that would have taken all the fun out of it.

Even though it was the middle of the day, there were barely any cars on the road. He coasted along, releasing the handlebars, and gently guided the bike around the windy curves with his knees. There was something meditative about riding like that, above it all, like he was the only one in the entire city.

Beep! Beep!

He quickly glanced behind his shoulder and saw a black SUV slowly following behind. Seeing there was no oncoming traffic, he waved his left arm, signaling for it to pass.

The car pulled up next to him and the passenger window rolled down. It was Celeste.

"Need a ride?"

"Very funny."

She sped up a little, but Charlie kept pace. "So this is what you do on that bike all day long."

"Should I be worried that you're stalking me, Celeste?" Charlie teased.

"Don't flatter yourself." A car pulled up behind them and tapped on the horn. "Follow me."

Before he could protest, she had pulled away and sped up, but she made sure never to be so far ahead that he couldn't see her. A few miles down she turned left onto a dirt road marked PRIVATE and followed it several hundred yards to where it ended at what could only be described as an estate. It looked like a sprawling stone English manor, only it was surrounded by lemon, orange, and avocado trees.

"What is this place?" Charlie asked.

"My dad's," Celeste said, heading toward the front gate.

Charlie didn't move and just stood there, holding his bike.

"Don't worry, no one's home. He and wife number three are in Bora-Bora—or some other tropical paradise."

The front door opened out onto a giant, high-ceilinged foyer that felt like it belonged more in a hotel lobby than the entrance to a home. Celeste walked diagonally across, past a gurgling fountain, through some French doors, and into an industrial-size kitchen that had multiple stoves and refrigerators.

"How many people live here?"

"One or two, depending on whether he's going through a divorce or not." Celeste grabbed a beer from the fridge. "Want one?"

"No, I'm good, thanks." She seemed so blasé about the whole thing, like she wasn't even talking about her own father.

"Come on, I'll give you the grand tour. Trust me, it's way more fun when he's not around."

She led the way to a bedroom that was even larger than the kitchen. It had a king-size bed in the middle, with low-lying tables next to it, and a giant flat-screen television that took up most of the back wall. The deck beyond had several lounge chairs and another fountain. "Master bedroom," she announced, "and there are about ten more just like it, so moving on."

They went through a door that took them out to a lush garden with every kind of flower imaginable. Just beyond, there was a pool with matching padded lounge chairs lined up on either side of it, and a cabana in the back that had a bar and a daybed inside. "Now this is why I come when he's not around," she said, dumping her bag in the cabana. "But we're not done yet. There's one more thing I want to show you."

He had no idea where she was taking him—and whether it was a good idea that he follow her—but he did anyway. They crossed the yard through a side door that led directly into a garage, which was bigger than his house. Five gleaming Porsches in five different colors stood parked in a row. Even the floor sparkled, like they'd walked into a private showroom for the über-rich.

"Pick one."

"Excuse me?"

"You heard me. Pick a color."

"Okay," Charlie said, a little uncertain. "Red."

Celeste opened a cabinet in the back, which housed a small safe. She punched in a few numbers and the door opened. "Same combination every time. It's just too easy." She reached in and took out a set of keys, tossing them to Charlie. "You can drive shift, right?"

"Clearly you don't like your dad, but that doesn't mean I want to be responsible for a hundred-thousand-dollar car. No way." He handed the keys back to her.

"Just admit it," Celeste said, dangling the keys in front of him. "You're intimidated. By the horsepower."

"Yeah, that's it," Charlie said.

"I think it is." She took a step closer and stared him down, twirling the key ring around her finger. "But I also think you should live a little. My dad will never know anyway, for whatever that's worth to you."

Whether it was the temptation of Mulholland's inviting, winding curves, or the sweet alluring scent of Celeste's perfume, Charlie snatched the keys back and pressed unlock. The car beeped twice and the lights flashed, like it was coming to life. "Get in."

"That's better," she said, sitting down on the passenger side.

Charlie slipped into the driver's seat and gripped the steering wheel. Checking out all the features on the dashboard, he thought it was just like being in a cockpit, with compact gauges and controls neatly aligned within reach, each with its defined purpose to optimize the performance of this finely tuned vehicle. He tapped his feet on the brakes, gas, and clutch, making sure they were all in the right place, and put the gear in neutral. Just as he was about to turn the key in the ignition, he heard a clanking noise coming from outside. "What was that?"

"I didn't hear anything. Let's go."

The clanking resumed. Now they both heard it.

"Shit. It's Wednesday, isn't it?" Celeste realized, getting out of the car. "Mission aborted," she whispered to Charlie. "It's Rosalinda."

"Your stepmother?"

She looked at him strangely. "No, the housekeeper."

A stout, gray-haired woman of about sixty who couldn't have been more than five feet tall greeted them when they got back to the kitchen.

"Ay! Celestina!" She embraced Celeste, muttering something in Spanish Charlie couldn't understand.

Celeste hugged her back and responded, also in Spanish, then pointed at Charlie, saying his name.

Rosalinda came up to him and gripped his arm with her coarse hand, staring up at him, repeating, "*Muy guapo*."

"What's she saying?" Charlie asked, unsure how to respond.

"She thinks you're handsome," Celeste explained. "Try not to let it go to your head."

He shot her a knowing look. "Coming from you, I'll take that under advisement."

A few minutes later a young Hispanic guy wearing headphones came into the kitchen holding a mop. His eyes lit up when he saw Celeste standing in front of him. "Wow. Look who's here."

"Don't I get a hug?" she asked, sauntering over to him.

The guy glanced over at Charlie before obliging.

Charlie stood awkwardly waiting for them to finish.

"Jose, this is Charlie, Charlie this is Jose. He's Rosalinda's grandson."

"Hanging by the pool since papa's away?" Jose asked.

"You know me too well. Come with us," she said, tugging on his sleeve. That seemed to be her signature move.

"Yeah, and you explain that to Rosalinda while she's slaving away on her own."

"Suit yourself," she said, unbuttoning her blouse, revealing a hot pink bikini top underneath. "You know where to find us. Ready?" she asked Charlie.

As soon as they got to the pool Celeste unbuttoned her shorts and shimmied them off by shaking her hips until they fell by her feet, leaving her in just her bikini. "That's better, don't you think?"

She stood in front of Charlie waiting for a response but he had nothing to say. He should have been drooling. He should have been playing "real or fake?" the way Teddy had instructed. After all, if Celeste was into it, who was he to argue?

But there was a problem. For some ridiculous reason—one completely incomprehensible to Charlie—there was nothing sexy about the way Celeste was standing there, practically naked, outside her father's empty mansion. Instead, it just reminded him of Sylvia and all the wrong reasons he had gone out with her in the first place.

"I'm going to take off."

"You can't leave. We just got here," Celeste stated plainly, like that was reason enough.

Charlie shrugged. "What can I say?" He started walking around the pool toward the house.

"Fine," Celeste said. "But I know where you live."

"That's right, you do," Charlie said, softening. "So I'll be seeing you."

• • •

Snowpeak99: hi.

Mollypop: hi back.

Snowpeak99: you're right on time.

Mollypop: yeah, i can't help it . . . makes me kind of uncool sometimes . . .

Snowpeak99: punctuality's an undervalued character trait.

Snowpeak99: so, i've been wondering . . . what's the deal with the stars?

Mollypop: what stars??

Snowpeak99: the ones on your ceiling. i'm staring up at them now. just turned out the lights so they're really glowing.

Mollypop: oh, those! i'm so used to them i forgot they were there. . . .

Mollypop: they were a gift from my dad.

Snowpeak99: are your parents divorced?

Mollypop: no, my dad died when i was seven.

Mollypop: he had cancer.

Snowpeak99: that's terrible. i'm really sorry, molly.

Mollypop: thanks . . .

Snowpeak99: tell me more about the stars. when did he give them to you?

Mollypop: on my sixth birthday. we got them together at the griffith park observatory . . . that massive white building with the round black dome at the top of the hill.

Snowpeak99: oh yeah—i've seen it.

Mollypop: we came home and i lay in bed telling him where to put them all. they've been in the same place ever since.

Snowpeak99: wow. so it's kind of like he's been watching over you all this time.

Mollypop: yeah . . . i suppose he has. i never really thought of it that way.

Snowpeak99: do you miss him?

Mollypop: yeah, i do.

Mollypop: nobody asks me that anymore. i guess since it happened so long ago, they just don't think about it or they don't want to bring it up or something.

Snowpeak99: people don't always know how to react to uncomfortable topics. take it from me, the son of lesbians.

Mollypop: what's that like?

Snowpeak99: it's all i know, so it seems normal to me. and boulder's a pretty liberal place. it's also small, so it's old news. that wasn't always the case, though.

Mollypop: what do you mean?

Snowpeak99: we were one of the first "planned" nontraditional families in boulder.

Snowpeak99: that's code for my moms went to a sperm bank and chose to have me.

Snowpeak99: it was more of a big deal back then cuz they were the first wave of lesbians doing it, so they got interviewed all the time.

Snowpeak99: all these strangers knew who i was and that my dad was a sperm donor and all this really private stuff.

Mollypop: wow . . . charlie, that's so intense.

Snowpeak99: yeah, it's kind of crazy. there were apparently people who hated me before i was even born.

Mollypop: i can't imagine being so . . . exposed.

Snowpeak99: i only found out all this stuff much later, so it wasn't such a big deal in the end. plus i live in a house with four girls—two of them are eleven—so privacy's kind of a foreign concept.

Snowpeak99: it's the 4th tomorrow.

Mollypop: yeah.

Snowpeak99: what are you doing?

Mollypop: i don't know yet . . . no plans . . . probably will go into the store.

Snowpeak99: isn't it closed?

Mollypop: yeah, but new stuff came in that i want to go through.

Snowpeak99: you work way too much. is it time for an intervention?

Mollypop: lol. you sound like my boss, penelope. i know it sounds dorky, but sorting through stuff relaxes me.

Snowpeak99: you're right, it does sound dorky, but i kind of get it.

Mollypop: well, thanks. now I can sleep calmly!!

Snowpeak99: yes, you can . . . it's getting late. i'll let you go.

Mollypop: good night, Charlie Richards.

Snowpeak99: good night, Molly Hill.

Love makes your soul crawl out from its hiding place.

—Zora Neale Hurston

Molly had fallen asleep with her laptop open on the bed next to her, and woke up in exactly the same position eight hours later. She reached over and touched the keyboard to wake up the sleeping computer.

There was a new e-mail from Charlie.

To: Molly
From: Charlie
Date: July 4, 2008 2:09 A.M. PST
Subject: To Do

M,

1. Clear your calendar. It's your DAY OFF! The store can wait.

2. Take my bike and follow the directions below.

3. Download this song and only press play when you get to the trail.

4. Get back to me when you're done.

You can thank me later.

C

She printed it out and looked at the instructions. He was sending her up a mountain. On a bike. There was no way she could do it. It had taken her a week to feel comfortable doing the same flat, easy route back and forth to the store every day. She wasn't ready for anything more challenging.

She got up and put on her bathrobe and went down for breakfast. Maybe Charlie was right about one thing, though—maybe she did need a day off. Maybe it was time that she at least made an effort with her mom and Ron instead of trying to avoid them.

She heard their voices downstairs and then the front door open.

"Mom! Wait!" Molly called out. "I'll come with you!"

But she heard the door close again before she could get all the words out.

She ran downstairs and peeked through the peephole, where she saw her mom walking down the front path, carrying a picnic basket, a cooler, and some beach towels. She had forgotten they were going to some lake for the day and wouldn't be back until dinnertime. They had invited her to join them but, like always, she had turned them down, claiming she had to work.

She could have followed them out and gotten them to wait for her, but she just stood there watching. Laura tripped over a pebble, dropping everything, when suddenly Ron entered the distorted round picture of the peephole to catch her amid the scattered blueberries, apples, and turkey sandwiches that seemed to spill out in slow motion. Laura let out a high-pitched squeal followed by girlish laughter as Ron steadied her. He bent down to check her laces, then swept her up in his arms and gallantly carried her to the car. It was weird seeing her mother that way—happy. For the first time, Molly realized that maybe they wanted to be alone and that she was actually doing them a favor by opting out. Maybe she wasn't punishing them with her absence at all. Maybe they preferred it that way.

She went back up to her room and plopped back down on the bed. A few minutes later she heard the distinctive sound of an incoming instant message. Since she wasn't expecting to hear from Charlie until later, it was likely Celeste. They had been in touch, but Molly felt a growing distance between them and had decided against telling her anything about Charlie. Celeste clearly didn't feel the need to share everything with Molly either, like the fact that she'd invited him—a so-called "dork"—to a party.

It turned out the IM wasn't from Celeste. It was from Rina. Finally! Molly had e-mailed her a week ago but hadn't heard anything back until now. Molly laughed. Did e-mail travel slower internationally?

DoctoRina: please tell me you're there and that you didn't just leave your laptop open...

Mollypop: reeeen!! i'm here, i'm here. you have no idea how happy i am to hear from you. where are you???

DoctoRina: in delhi. we just got here this afternoon. we were visiting my great-great-aunt or something in this small town and had no internet access . . . ugh . . . anyway, here i am. i just got your e-mail. so . . . tell me more about charlie!

Mollypop: well, he's expecting me to go mountain biking today up this trail he told me about, but there's no way i'm gonna do it.

DoctoRina: why not?? that sounds like so much fun.

Mollypop: i know you're in the adventurous spirit, being in india and all, but don't forget who you're talking to.

DoctoRina: you even said yourself in your e-mail how great it's been riding his bike.

Mollypop: tell me more about you. how was the wedding?

DoctoRina: amazing. my cousin was so incredibly beautiful. i still have the henna all over my hands and feet. my mom said she's going to teach me how to do it, so you'll be my first victim when we get back.

Mollypop: i'm so glad you're having such a great time. take lots of pictures for me.

DoctoRina: i will. oh—they have the most amazing fabric stores here. i've already picked out a special treat for you.

Mollypop: you're so sweet, reen. you always think of me.

DoctoRina: oops. i think i hear my dad coming down the hall. it's four in the morning and he'll kill me if he sees i'm still up. gotta go . . . love you!!!!

Molly was so happy to hear from Rina. She was a reminder that she wasn't so alone, that there were people out there who understood her, even if they were thousands of miles away.

She got up and threw off her robe. Rina would be mortified if she stayed in all day and moped. As she was getting dressed, she noticed her bulging suitcase at the back of the room. She walked over and opened it up, revealing the pile of Charlie's clothes she had dumped there almost three weeks before. She reached in and pulled out something yellow peeking out from underneath the pile. It was an old T-shirt with Colorado written across the front in faded navy blue letters. She held it up to her nose and breathed in, wondering if that was what Charlie smelled like.

She slipped it on over her tank top, gathered her things, and set out on her ride.

Molly followed the directions a few miles down Boulder Canyon Boulevard and then made a few quick rights until she was at the entrance to the Betasso Canyon loop. She had already ridden much longer than she anticipated just *getting* there. She contemplated turning around, but she wasn't tired, and all that was waiting for her was an empty house. A few riders had just set out ahead of her, so if anything went wrong, she at least wouldn't be stranded alone.

After experimenting with the gears, she settled into a slow, comfortable rhythm and relaxed enough to look up from the ground. She had been so focused on avoiding overturned rocks that she hadn't noticed that the trail had leveled out into a meadow of grass on either side of her.

She suddenly remembered the song Charlie had sent and took out her iPod and pressed play. The rhythmic beat of The Arcade Fire's "No Cars Go" built in intensity as she stared out at the narrow path that gradually ascended as far as she could see.

Okay, this isn't so bad, she thought, clipping her feet back into the pedals. *I can do this.*

She cycled across the field until it narrowed and hugged the side of the mountain, then widened again, taking her through various pockets of dense forest.

The farther she went, the more she could feel every muscle in her body tighten and snap. She had no idea where her energy was coming from. As much as her brain kept telling her to turn around, her heart compelled her forward. With each steep turn and difficult ascent, she pretended Charlie was right behind her, encouraging her, urging her to prove what she was really made of.

When the song ended, she hit repeat and played it over until the trail looped back to where she'd begun.

Molly rode back home with the song still playing. As soon as she got to the house she ran upstairs and pulled her notebook out of her laptop bag. She had shoved it in with the internship folder at the last second. She plugged her iPod into the stereo. With no one home she could play it as loud as she wanted. She listened to Charlie's song again and started to draw.

• • •

From: Molly
To: Charlie
Date: July 4, 3:33 P.M. MST
Subject: No Cars Go

C,

I did it! Surprised? What can I say—I'm so glad you convinced me. It was the most amazing experience ever. Smart move too, not telling me how far away it was. If I'd known, not to mention how narrow that trail gets (especially when it goes around the side of the mountain), I'm sure I would have chickened out. But once you're there, you have no choice but to just go in one direction, and I was just doing it!!! I couldn't believe it was me! I felt like I was so far away from . . . EVERYTHING . . . lost in the middle of nature.

I was so excited I practically flew all the way back. It must have only taken like fifteen minutes compared to what felt like an hour getting there.

Have I mentioned how much I LOVED the song? I only listened to it a million times. I played it on the stereo when I got back. I was so inspired I just started sketching. I literally just stopped and here I am, e-mailing you.

THANK YOU for the best Fourth of July ever!! I wish I could return the favor. The best I can do is direct you to the nearest fireworks. They have an awesome show at the snobby golf club a few blocks away on Beverly. My mom and I walk over every year after dinner. You get the best view if you stand outside the gates on the sidewalk. This is one event that they can't make "members only." Tons of people do it, so get there early for a good spot. When the fireworks erupt, you feel so close you expect them to rain back down on you.

M

P.S. I really don't know how to thank you. It was a relief to feel like myself again.

Charlie read Molly's e-mail again. For a supposedly private person, she was refreshingly open and honest. He could practically feel her energy bouncing off the screen. It was a sensation he knew well and often experienced after riding the Boulder trails. The ability to let go like that, he believed, to really give yourself over to the ride, had nothing to do with being a good athlete. It was all about the capacity to focus, to know how to shut out the rest of the world except for your immediate surroundings. Somehow, he knew Molly could do that.

He thought back to his first night and how everything in the room had blended together in an indistinguishable wash of pastels. All he could think about then was how he didn't want to be there. Now it was the only place he wanted to be.

He stood in front of the corkboard and scanned it for pictures of Molly. He thought he'd spotted them all, but every now and then a new one seemed to appear. This time a Polaroid of her asleep on a beach next to Celeste revealed itself. Initially only her black hair was visible, like she had deliberately covered it with another picture so that she'd be obscured.

She was even more mysterious with her eyes closed, like she was aware of something that no one else could see.

It made him want to get closer, to be able to touch her.

He examined the series of sketches taped to the wall behind the sewing machine. Now that he was paying close attention, he realized that they were all drawings of the same dress but at different stages. They looked like they'd been drawn by the confident hand of someone who'd done it thousands of time before.

Charlie opened the closet and ran his hand along the row of dresses, neatly arranged by color, hanging from the rack. Which ones had Molly made? He pulled out a bright green silk dress that wrapped around the middle with a bow. He took it off the rack and held it out into the light, comparing it to the sketches, discovering that it was the same dress. Just to make sure, he looked at the collar and read the tag. It read MOLLY HILL.

"What are you doing?"

Charlie turned around and saw Mia standing there waiting for an answer. He was still holding the green dress. "What are *you* doing in my room?"

"Charlie's trying on a dress!" she hollered at the top of her lungs, and raced out before Charlie could catch her.

"Great," he yelled back. "Announce it to the neighborhood."

• • •

They heard the fireworks from the house and could see them the second they turned onto Beverly. Charlie had told his moms about them, and they decided it would be a fun family outing. The girls ran ahead in excitement while Charlie walked along with Sally and Lisa.

"I'm so glad you suggested this," Sally said.

"Me too." They walked along in companionable silence. It had been a while since he had been alone with them.

"We hardly see you," Sally added, tousling his hair. "I hope that means you've been having a good time."

"It's been okay, actually," Charlie admitted.

"It looks like you and Celeste have been getting along," Lisa observed. This was her not-so-subtle way of probing for information.

"There's nothing going on, if that's what you're getting at."

"I wasn't implying anything," she said, smirking.

"That's right, she *wasn't*." Sally threw a warning glance Lisa's way.

If Lisa had it her way, he would tell her *everything*, especially about his love life. He often did, but this time he didn't know how to explain that the main thing holding him back from Celeste was Molly. How could his mother understand something like that when it barely made sense to him?

• • •

They caught up to Heather and Mia at the corner directly across from the club, where a handful of other families had set up chairs and coolers. All you could see was the high brick wall until the fireworks shot up hundreds of feet into the air.

Farther down the sidewalk Charlie noticed Celeste sitting on the curb. She didn't turn to talk to anyone and stared up at the exploding sky. His first instinct was to quickly look the other way, to avoid any further questions from Lisa, but when he glanced back, he noticed that she was alone. She seemed different when she thought no one was looking, not so guarded or haughty. If anything, she seemed lonely.

"I'll be right back." He pushed through the thickening crowd. "Hey! Celeste!"

"Oh, hi," she said, flustered. "I'm meeting some people, but I must have lost them," she explained, standing up. "Pretty lame display, huh?"

The sky erupted into a flash of purple, green, and orange. There was nothing lame about it. "I think it's kind of beautiful," he said.

She turned and stared at Charlie. "Let's crash the party at the golf club," she finally said.

He looked back toward his parents and sisters in the crowd, then at Celeste. The easy thing, the obvious thing, would be to go with her. "They're expecting me," he finally said, pointing out his family. "Come join us?"

"Pass," she said, walking away in the other direction. "I have to find my friends anyway."

Gravitation cannot be held responsible for people falling in love. How on earth can you explain in terms of chemistry and physics so important a biological phenomenon as first love? Put your hand on a stove for a minute and it seems like an hour. Sit with that special girl for an hour and it seems like a minute. That's relativity.

—Albert Einstein

"I was right."

"About what?" Molly asked, coming over to the desk where Penelope was sorting through the mail.

"That you needed a day off." She peered at Molly over her reading glasses. "It's like you're a different person."

"People don't change in a day," she said, rolling her eyes.

"That all depends, honey. What's his name?"

"I have no idea what you're talking about." Molly turned around and busied herself hanging some clothes. She knew her expression would be a dead giveaway.

"You don't have to tell me, but you have five hours left in your shift. Think you can hide that grin all day?"

It was a losing battle. Penelope was right and she couldn't hide it. She turned around and sat down next to her. "Is it that obvious?"

"Only in a good way."

"The thing is, it's complicated," Molly began.

"How so?"

"Well, for starters, we've never met and probably never will."

"All right, honey," Penelope said, putting the mail aside and removing her glasses. "Now I'm confused."

Molly explained the whole situation, how she was staying in Charlie's room and he was in hers, how they'd been writing more and more, and how Molly had never felt that close to anyone before.

"That's possibly the most romantic thing I've ever heard," Penelope said when Molly was done.

"You really think so?" It was a relief to get it all off her chest and to be able to talk about it with someone right in front of her.

"Who writes letters anymore? I'm telling you, it's the best way to fall in love."

"They're not exactly letters," Molly corrected her.

"Close enough," Penelope said.

"He knows you, actually," Molly confessed.

"Well, honey, who is he?"

"Charlie Richards. He told me he shops here sometimes."

"You're staying at the Richardses'? Why didn't I know this before? They are the most wonderful family, especially that Charlie. Now I understand why you're grinning."

Molly felt a sense of relief that she had been right to trust her instincts instead of the words of a jilted ex-girlfriend. Penelope had been living in Boulder so long, Molly figured she was one of the people who'd read about the Richardses in the newspaper before Charlie was born. But that wasn't what Penelope meant. She was referring to the fact that Charlie was a good person. And that he was hot. Hot enough to break the hearts of beautiful girls like Sylvia. "It's kind of pointless. I mean, he can have any girl he wants."

"But he's writing to you. And I'm not surprised. I can see how you two would get along. Maybe it's his family situation, but that boy has a sensitivity I've rarely seen. He has an old soul, just like you."

Without realizing it, Molly had inched her chair closer so that she and Penelope were practically touching. It was reassuring hearing about Charlie from someone who knew him. It made her feel less insecure about trusting him, a total stranger.

"What's this?" Penelope lifted Molly's sketchbook from beneath the pile of mail.

Molly had been drawing when Penelope went on her morning coffee run and mistakenly left it there. "It's nothing," she said, slipping the book into her purse.

"I see. Just more of your doodling, right?"

Molly didn't know that Penelope had seen her drawings, but before she could answer, the front door jingled. It was Laura.

"Mom? Hi," she said on her way to greet her. "What are you doing here?"

"Hi, Molls. I hope I'm not bothering you, but we were in town and wanted to see if we could take you for lunch. Ron's just looking for parking."

Molly looked back to Penelope.

"Go on. I'll hold down the fort."

"Are you sure?" She didn't know what she'd talk about with Ron during a whole meal, but she needed to eat.

"Molly, you've already done enough to last me several months. Go enjoy yourself."

"I love the new display, Molls," Laura said, taking in the mannequins now dressed in completely different outfits. "When did you change it?"

"Last week." Now that she was more familiar with the inventory, she had several outfits prepared for window rotation every week. This was already her third display.

"You have quite a daughter," Penelope said. "Her smart thinking has brought in so much more business. Customers think we're constantly getting new merchandise—and selling out of it. It's been a revolving door around here ever since Molly arrived."

Molly blushed and adjusted the belt on one of the mannequins. "That's a slight exaggeration," she said.

"A surefire way to make Molly work harder is to give her a compliment," Laura joked. "She's like her dad that way."

Molly winced. She'd said it so casually, like he wasn't dead, like *he* was the one out there looking for a parking spot. "My real dad," Molly clarified.

A silence fell over the room, and she immediately regretted saying it, even before she noticed her mother's eye twitch the way it always did when her feelings were hurt. She was about to say something, to try and take it back, when the door jingled again.

"Sorry it took so long," Ron announced, entering the store. "Hi, you must be Penelope," he said, walking over to shake her hand. "I'm Ron."

• • •

Molly followed a few paces behind as they made their way down the Pearl Street Mall. Strangers passing by thought they were just a regular family enjoying a beautiful day like everyone else.

"Where should we go?" Ron asked, slowing down so Molly could catch up. "I haven't been here in years, so you're the expert."

"There's a good Italian place just down there," Molly said, pointing to a green awning over a cluster of tables on the sidewalk. She had been there once before. The food was okay, but the key was that it came quickly.

"That sounds perfect," Laura said, pulling Molly closer so she could walk between them the rest of the way.

When they got there, the host sat them inside, but Ron insisted on the last available table on the sidewalk patio where they could have a view of the crowds streaming by.

The waiter arrived with the menus and two wineglasses, which he placed in front of Ron and Laura. "We'll be needing three glasses," Ron corrected, in a confident tone to stave off any questions about Molly's age.

"Right away, sir," the waiter said.

"I was thinking white. Is that okay with you?" he asked, directing the question at Molly.

Molly was caught off guard. She had stopped feeling like anything approaching an adult now that she was officially the third wheel. Working at the store at least made her feel like she was her own person, not some annoying tagalong. "I better not," Molly finally said. "I have to get back to work."

Ron consulted Laura next and ordered a half-bottle of chardonnay. Ron poured Molly's glass first when the bottle arrived. "Just a small taste," he said. "So you can join in the toast."

Molly's stomach tightened into small knots. The last time Ron had made a toast, her life had been turned upside down.

"To summer," he said, clinking his glass against Laura's. Molly obliged and raised hers too. "And to wine in the middle of the afternoon."

Molly took a sip of the wine once the waiter had taken their orders. The only alcohol she usually liked was beer, which Celeste advised she keep to herself, since it was so uncouth, but this tasted pretty good.

"Your mom told me you went mountain biking," Ron said.

"I just went up a trail. It wasn't that far." She knew he was just trying to be friendly, but there was no way she could explain the way the ride had made her feel when she didn't feel comfortable talking to him about something as simple as the weather.

"I miss riding trails," he said, taking another sip from his glass.

Molly looked up, surprised. "You do?"

Ron nodded. "I used to do it every summer growing up. My parents traveled so much that once school let out they'd drop me off at my grandfather's farm in Vermont for a couple of months. There's only so much lawn mowing and cow milking a kid can take, so I'd spend hours up on the trails."

She had never thought about Ron as a real person, with parents and a grandfather and a past in the hills of Vermont. Only as someone she'd have to tolerate for the rest of her life. This new information was . . . interesting.

"Well, why haven't you been riding here?" she asked. "I mean, there's practically a trail in our backyard."

"I haven't ridden since my last summer there, right before I began my freshman year of college. My grandfather died in the middle of my parents' divorce, so the farm got sold in the process and I never got to go back."

Laura reached for Ron's hand. "I never knew that, honey. Molly's right. You should try it again here."

Molly swallowed. She felt guilty for so readily dismissing Ron when he clearly had memories and feelings just like she did. Maybe—maybe she could try just a little bit harder. "I'm sure Charlie wouldn't mind if you borrowed one of his bikes," she offered. "He left a note saying we could use them all summer," she added, trying to cover how she knew this.

"Maybe you two can go together sometime," Laura suggested.

"I'd love that," Ron said, but with the waiter arriving at the same time with their food, Molly pretended she didn't hear him.

"I better take mine to go," she said, looking at her watch. "I'm sure Penelope's waiting for me."

• • •

To: Charlie
From: Molly
Date: July 7, 5:29 P.M. MST
Subject: stuff

I really miss my dad today. It'll pass, but it just hits me out of the blue sometimes. I feel like you're the only person I could share that with. . . .

Heading up to the Betasso Loop with my notebook. Going to try drawing up there.

Hope you're having a great day.

M

• • •

Molly was right. Charlie had seen the observatory on his rides in Griffith Park—it was hard to miss—but he had never been inside. He turned off the trail onto a road that stretched, like a runway, to the imposing white domed building at the end, perched on the Los Angeles side of the mountain overlooking the city.

Once the road ended, a well-tended lawn took over, divided by a paved path in the middle. Even though he'd never been to Washington, it reminded him of pictures he'd seen of the National Mall. He locked his bike to a post and walked down the path, past a large sculpture called *Astronomers Monument*, depicting busts of famous scientists like Newton and Galileo. In front was a sundial, whose shadow accurately determined that it was eight minutes to six. Just outside the entrance a series of concentric circles was engraved in the ground, each corresponding to the various planetary orbits around the sun.

As he walked toward the stairs leading to the doors, a guard stopped him. "I'm sorry, sir, we're closing at six tonight for a private event."

Charlie looked at his watch, then back at the guard. "Can I just go to the gift shop? I'll be out in five minutes, I promise. I know what I'm getting."

"I'm not supposed to let anyone else in."

Charlie slumped his shoulders and started to turn around.

"You have four minutes," the guard whispered, taking pity on him. "And go down over there," he said, pointing out a staircase that looked like it went down right into the canyon below. "It'll take you right to the gift shop."

"Thanks. I'll be out in three." He ran across the lawn and down the steps two at a time, through a door on the left that took him right to the store.

Luckily it was empty, making it easier to scan the aisles even faster. Charlie hadn't been lying; he did know exactly what he was looking for, and he finally found it hanging from a twirling display near the cashier: a packet of glow-in-the-dark adhesive stars.

"Anything else?" the guy behind the counter asked.

He had his head down toward the cash register, but when he looked up, Charlie recognized him immediately. "Hey, you're Jose, right?" Jose looked at him, blank. "Charlie. I met you the other day with Celeste."

At the mention of her name, Jose's expression softened. "Oh, hey. Sorry, man. I see thousands of faces here all day. They kind of blend together. Is Celeste with you?"

"No, I'm here alone."

Jose rang him up and handed him his bag and receipt. "We're closed now, so I'll walk out with you."

"This place looks amazing," Charlie commented when they reached the top of the stairs. Since the observatory was perched at the edge of the mountain, it provided a panoramic view of the L.A. basin.

"You didn't check it out?" Jose asked, surprised.

"Only had time for this," Charlie explained, holding up the bag with the stickers. "I'm definitely coming back."

"They for your girl?" Jose asked. "The stickers," he added, reading the confusion on Charlie's face. "Chicks love that kind of thing. I've been working here for ten months, so you pick up stuff like that."

"I'm not really sure what she is," he said.

"No shame, bro. Most dudes in Celeste's world feel that way."

"Oh, they're not for Celeste. She's just my temporary neighbor for the summer," Charlie clarified. "I usually live in Boulder and they're for . . . someone there."

"Ah, well, Celeste thrives on competition, so watch out," Jose joked.

"She doesn't know about any of this so, you know—"

"I got it," Jose interrupted. "I won't say anything." He walked over to the left. "Come on. You gotta at least check this out since you came all this way."

He was standing on a bronze-plated line that ran diagonally across the patio toward the railing. "What is it?" Charlie asked.

"Sunset lines. You see, they run all the way across here and tell you where the sun is going to set depending on the time of year, give or take."

Charlie walked over to the summer solstice line, which almost exactly lined up with the position of the sun, since it had only just happened a couple weeks before. The sun hovered in the sky, on its way down, to the left of the Hollywood sign. He'd never understood why people cared so much and made pilgrimages to see it, but from this vantage point the oversize square white letters seemed almost majestic, like they belonged there.

"Cool, huh?"

"Yeah, totally," Charlie said, snapping out of his trance.

As they walked back toward the street, Charlie stopped at the post where he had locked his bike. "This is me."

Jose came closer to check it out. "A Stumpie," he said, taking note of the brand. "Wow. It's the new FSR Comp. Nice, man. How's it ride?"

"It's awesome," Charlie said, perking up. "Really agile and smooth. You cycle?"

"Yeah, my ride's down there. Give me a second and I can show you some killer trails."

Jose came back a few minutes later on a customized Stumpjumper from the late nineties. The wheels were pimped with chrome rims, just like on a car, and the frame was a dull black with STUMPIE spray-painted across it in a rainbow of graffiti letters. "Follow me."

He headed down a steep path off the main road and Charlie followed, past hikers and people walking their dogs. About a quarter mile along, he cut off the main trail onto a narrow, densely wooded path that led back up the hill. Jose looked back a couple of times to make sure Charlie was keeping up.

"All good," Charlie yelled out, giving him the thumbs-up signal the next time he looked back. He thought he had already covered the park's fifty-two miles of trails, but now it felt like Jose was leading him into the heart of the mountain. The deeper in they went, the rougher the terrain, but they charged up faster, feeding off each other's energy.

They rode along like that for a while, switching off the lead when the trail was wide enough. It had been a while since Charlie had ridden with anyone. It was usually such a solitary experience but it was exhilarating doing it with Jose, on new ground. He felt his heart beat, muscles flex, and lungs expand just a bit more, reminding him what he was made of as they pushed each other forward.

It was a light drop at first, which Charlie mistook as sweat flying off his face, but more followed in quick succession until the clouds exploded with thunder. A few minutes later the sky grew dark and sheets of rain came pouring down on them. The mud trail softened almost instantly, but with a few quick gear shifts, neither of them slowed down.

They were on their way down now, wet mud and rain splashing out as they picked up speed. Almost without warning the trail evened out and spilled out on the other side of the park.

"That was sick, man," Jose said when they stopped at the bottom. He biked up to Charlie and gave him a high five, their wet hands slapping together.

"You know these trails," Charlie said, catching his breath.

"It's practically my backyard, dude."

With the rain coming down so hard, Charlie had lost his bearings. "Where exactly are we?"

"Welcome to the East Side. Why don't you come over and wait out this rain? It'll be a bitch for you to get home now. L.A. driving goes to shit when it rains." A car whizzing past honked. "See what I mean?"

Charlie looked down at his soaked shirt sticking against him and his mud-splattered legs. The stickers were the only things that had managed to stay dry, thanks to their plastic packaging. "Thanks, man. That'd be great."

• • •

"You can bring it in here," Jose said, wheeling his bike down a dark corridor. It had only taken them five minutes to get to his place, just off a busy avenue called Alvarado. Once they'd hit the main roads, Charlie had reoriented himself and realized they were just a few miles east of Molly's house, but they might as well have been hundreds. He had heard that L.A. was almost half Hispanic, but hadn't had any sense of how true that was until he got to Jose's neighborhood. Every billboard, storefront, and sign was suddenly in Spanish, the buses were packed, and actual *pedestrians*, dozens of them, lined the sidewalks even though it was raining. It was the first time he felt like he was in a real city.

They walked up four flights and passed other apartments, many with their doors open as if it was a communal building. Spanish was the only language spoken.

"You remember my grandma," Jose said, opening the door to apartment 4D.

Before he could answer, Rosalinda rushed toward them, holding out towels as though she had anticipated Jose's soggy return, the whole time speaking so fast

Charlie wouldn't have been able to understand her even if it were in English.

She turned to Charlie next, wrapping the towel around his shoulders and guiding him toward the hall. Jose took over and led him to a bedroom in the back. It had a bed and a nightstand containing a lamp, a Bible, and rosary beads. They walked around the screen where there was another bed, a few Spanish posters on the wall, and a dresser.

Jose took out a hooded sweatshirt and a pair of jeans and handed them to Charlie. "You can wear these for now," he said. "I'm going to shower. When you're ready, Rosalinda will give you something to eat."

Once he was changed, Charlie went back down the hall to the kitchen.

"*Tenga, para usted*," Rosalinda said, handing him a steaming cup of hot chocolate.

Charlie took a sip and gasped. This hot chocolate was . . . spicy? Rosalinda smiled and held up a bunch of chilies. "Very good," she said, shaking them. "Very good for you."

He sat down and warmed his hands around the mug, while his mouth recovered from the chilies. He watched Rosalinda scurry around the kitchen, sprinkling flour over the counter and rolling out a giant mound of dough. He used to love helping Lisa bake when he was a kid. Sally rarely set foot in the kitchen except to refill her coffee.

"Come," Rosalinda said, motioning for him to stand next to her. She demonstrated how to tear off a chunk of dough, sprinkle it with flour, and spread it out with the rolling pin. Once it was flat, she cut it into triangles and placed them on a greased tray next to her. "You," she said, when she was done, and walked over to another counter, where she began cutting fresh pieces of pineapple.

Charlie didn't really know what he was doing but he got to work, smoothing out the dough and cutting it into shapes that approximated the triangle. A few minutes later, she came back to check on him.

"*Bueno*," she said approvingly, rubbing his cheek with the back of her hand. It was such an intimate gesture, especially from a stranger, but it felt good. Charlie had never known any of his grandparents, but he imagined this was what it would have been like if he had.

"You a good boy," Rosalinda said, gazing up at him.

"Thank you. *Gracias*," Charlie said, which was the extent of his Spanish.

"Celeste, she much, much happier now because she meet you."

Charlie wanted to ask Rosalinda what she meant or how she knew that, but the language barrier was too big to get any of it across.

She divvied the pineapple chunks out onto the cut pieces of dough, sprinkled them with an orange-colored syrup, and folded the triangles over before placing them in the oven to brown.

"Don't hold your breath, *Abuelita*," Jose said, arriving in an outfit almost identical to Charlie's. "He's not in love with her. *El ama otra*."

Rosalinda smiled knowingly and pinched Charlie's cheek.

"What'd you say to her?" Charlie asked Jose.

"I just told her what you don't know yet."

"And what's that?" Charlie asked, gripping his mug.

"That you're in love with someone else."

• • •

Snowpeak99: there you are.

Mollypop: hi! how was your day?

Snowpeak99: i discovered that contrary to popular belief, it does rain in L.A.

Mollypop: yeah . . . like twice a year!

Snowpeak99: i also discovered pinkberry.

Snowpeak99: correction. i was dragged there by my little sisters.

Mollypop: and?

Snowpeak99: can you please explain what the big deal is?

Mollypop: nope, sorry. i don't get it either. i'm an old-fashioned ice cream girl myself.

Snowpeak99: favorite flavor?

Mollypop: toss-up between rocky road or vanilla, mood depending. yours?

Snowpeak99: interesting.

Snowpeak99: i'm a pralines 'n' cream man when it's available.

Mollypop: hmmm . . . sophisticated.

Snowpeak99: your sketches are amazing, btw.

Snowpeak99: the ones on the wall.

Mollypop: oh . . . thanks.

Snowpeak99: hope you don't mind. i took a closer look.

Mollypop: no, i don't mind at all. . . . i'm just embarrassed cuz no one ever really sees them.

Snowpeak99: do you realize how talented you are?

Mollypop: now you're really embarrassing me!

Snowpeak99: you're too modest.

Mollypop: you don't know that! we've never met. . . .

Snowpeak99: but i'm right. admit it.

Mollypop: okay . . . maybe a little.

Snowpeak99: you should get paid to do it. that's how good you are.

Mollypop: ha! thanks . . . i wouldn't go that far, but i was going to apply for an internship in the fall with my favorite designer.

Snowpeak99: and did you?

Mollypop: i ended up changing my mind.

Snowpeak99: how come?

Mollypop: i don't know, really. . . . when i found out we were coming here for the summer, it didn't seem like i'd be able to do it so i kind of just gave up.

Snowpeak99: is it too late to change your mind?

Mollypop: yeah . . . the deadline's august 1.

Snowpeak99: that's still more than three weeks away. you have to go for it, molly.

Snowpeak99: you can win it. i know you can.

Mollypop: i'll think about it. . . .

Snowpeak99: what's holding you back?

Mollypop: i don't know . . . it's like, i'm not used to anyone seeing my work. . . . it feels so personal.

Snowpeak99: but you have to go for it—you have to put it out there and believe that other people will see how talented you are.

Mollypop: i know you're right. . . . it's just hard to let go sometimes. to trust that everything's going to be all right.

Snowpeak99: letting go is when you have the most fun.

Snowpeak99: you just can't think about it too much. it's like riding downhill.

Mollypop: i can't believe i'm telling you all this. . . .

123

Snowpeak99: i'm glad you are. it's nice to talk about real things for a change.

Mollypop: yeah, it is.

Mollypop: btw, do you compete in bike races? i was wondering because of those trophies in your cabinet . . . impressive!

Snowpeak99: thanks. they're from a couple of years ago when i used to race, but i stopped.

Mollypop: why? you were obviously really good.

Snowpeak99: it wasn't fun anymore and started to feel more like a job in a way, so i decided to quit.

Mollypop: wow. just like that? do you miss it?

Snowpeak99: no. once i make up my mind about something, i can just kind of move on.

Snowpeak99: it's so much better now because i just go out riding whenever i feel like it, wherever i feel like going, and i don't have to worry about a training schedule or checking my pace or any of that other stuff.

Mollypop: so now you just do it because you love it.

Snowpeak99: exactly. i've gotten really into exploring new trails.

Mollypop: you mean trails you've never been on before?

Snowpeak99: trails no one's been on. i've been riding off-trail and forging new ones.

Snowpeak99: i've made so many now that i started mapping them in this leather journal i bought.

Mollypop: charlie, that's the coolest thing i've ever heard.

Snowpeak99: well, thanks. i've gotten really into it. i was actually planning on spending the summer doing it.

Snowpeak99: i think that wins the dork contest.

Mollypop: please. you're talking to a girl who spends her day sorting clothes.

Mollypop: so i guess the house swap wasn't on your agenda either.

Snowpeak99: nope. it wasn't.

Snowpeak99: but it's turning out to be a really good summer.

Mollypop: yeah . . . i think so too.

Too many things are occurring for even a big heart to hold.

—W.B. Yeats

"Hi, Mom," Molly said, coming into the kitchen after work. A vase of fresh flowers stood in the middle of the table.

"Well, look who's here," Laura said, taking a tray out of the oven. "Just in time for some brownies. Oh, and this just came for you." She handed Molly a small padded envelope.

Molly took one of the warm brownies and sat down to open the package. Her stomach fluttered when she recognized the return address in the left-hand corner: it was her own.

It was from Charlie.

She put the brownie back, took the envelope, and stood up. "I'm going to change first, then I'll be back down."

She ran up the stairs, taking two at a time, gripping the envelope between her fingers. She got to her room and sat in the middle of the floor, just like she always did in her own bedroom on the shag carpet, and opened it. A

card and a small, thin, flat package, gift wrapped in colorful balloon paper, spilled out. She read the card first.

M
So you always have your stars.
P.S. You have my permission to put them on my ceiling.
C

Her heart started beating faster as she carefully unwrapped the package. She was dying to tear it open, but she held back to savor every moment. She had never gotten a gift or a card or anything in the mail before from a boy. She removed the final piece of tape, revealing a packet of glow-in-the-dark stickers, almost exactly the same kind her father had bought her all those years before.

Her heart stopped. She felt a well of tears spring up, but they got caught somewhere in her tightening throat, unable to come out. She suddenly couldn't breathe. *What's happening to me?* She took a deep breath, trying to dislodge the tears, but it only made it worse. She looked back down at the packet of stars and picked them up. Holding them in her hand, she read Charlie's note again. It was the only thing that calmed her. He was the only one who could calm her.

Her lungs reopened, and a big breath came out, followed by a slow stream of tears, only she wasn't sad at all—she was happy. That's when it hit her, when she finally figured out what was really going on: she was falling in love.

She looked back at the locked drawer, then at the shoe box on top of the bookcase containing the key. She was dying to know more about Charlie,

to know *everything* about him. **Especially** now, with her heart so full of longing. Besides their e-mails **and instant** messages, this room and what was in it were Molly's only real connection to him, the only tangible things of his she could touch.

She got up and carried the desk chair over to the bookcase. She hoisted herself up, reached for the box, and rummaged around inside it until she felt the key. She put it in the lock but hesitated before turning it. She knew that it was wrong, that she of all people should know the value of privacy, but she couldn't help herself. She turned the key until the lock clicked and pulled the drawer open.

There was nothing there. Just some old mail and magazines it seemed like Charlie had swept in there at the last minute to be sorted and tossed when he got back. All that buildup for nothing. Part of her was relieved—she didn't much like the idea of prying—but a bigger part of her felt disappointed. She had wanted to find something, *anything* to bring her closer to Charlie.

She was about to close the drawer and lock it up again when she noticed the corner of a photograph peeking out from the back. She reached in and pulled it out.

It was a picture of Sylvia and Charlie. She felt a few quick jealous pangs seeing him in the arms of another girl but at least it was over between them. She was certain of that. More important, Charlie was hot. And not just in the eye-of-the-beholder way. No, Charlie was hotter than that. He was the most handsome guy she had ever laid eyes on, even if it was only a picture.

Molly pulled the drawer open wider where there was a loose, spilled pile of more photographs. She had been wondering why Charlie didn't have any pictures of his friends anywhere in his room; now she'd finally found them.

She grabbed a handful and sat down.

Oh. My. God. Her insides tightened as she flipped through them. Charlie had his arm around a different girl in every picture, each girl just as pretty if not prettier than the next. The corners of the photographs were bent and indented, like they had each spent time in the empty frame on his desk.

The sense of elation she had felt moments before was replaced with a leaden heart. She was furious with herself for having opened up so much, for even *thinking* she had a chance with him, for letting herself get so carried away. It was foolish and unlike her and she should have listened to Sylvia because she was right—Charlie was a player, and players never changed.

She collected the pictures off the floor and put them back in the drawer. She was about to close it when she suddenly picked up the card and packet of stickers and put them in too. She shut the drawer tight before locking it and returning the key.

• • •

"You're sure it's going to come off?" Charlie asked the tattoo artist, who was hunched over her stool, putting the finishing touches on the lotus flower she had drawn on Mia's wrist. She had already completed Heather's, also a lotus flower. There was no hesitation in making their decision—they both wanted that exact tattoo because it matched the permanent one on Celeste's left ankle.

"Oh, just chill, Mr. Mountain Man," Celeste interjected. "It's henna. They'll wash off in two days, three max, right?"

"Totally," the artist said. Her matted, dreadlocked hair was pulled back in a purple tie-dyed bandanna, and her hands were covered in a delicate, intricate pattern in the same orange henna she'd used on Charlie's sisters. "That's the beauty of it. Nothing's permanent."

They were in the middle of the Venice boardwalk, surrounded by burning incense, street musicians, and vendors like this tattoo artist, selling everything from healing stones to paintings of the view in front of them—the Pacific Coast. Charlie had expected to hear this kind of spiritual jargon here but for some reason what the tattoo artist said made him think about Molly. He wondered if she'd gotten the stars yet; it had already been three days since he'd mailed them.

"See? You might just have to learn to trust me," Celeste said.

"You just love the hero worship," Charlie teased.

"This might be a good time to remind you that you asked to join us."

That wasn't entirely accurate. Celeste had already been taking his sisters to the beach and she'd asked Charlie if he wanted to come. It was the hottest day of the summer so he said yes. "That's when I thought we were going to the beach. You know, the sand, the water. Right next to it wasn't what I had in mind."

"So impatient!" Celeste chastised.

When Mia's tattoo was finished, they resumed walking along the boardwalk. A few blocks down, Charlie could see what looked like an outdoor gym—literally an entire gym—outside. "What *is* that?"

"Muscle Beach," Celeste explained as they approached.

"Fitting name." It had every kind of free weight imaginable, along with about a dozen extremely built, oversize men lifting them—teeth gritting, veins popping on full display. Charlie had never seen anyone that muscular in person, only in those power-lifting competitions he occasionally saw while flipping channels on TV.

Heather scrunched her nose in disgust. "Ewww. It's so gross!"

"That's what you look like, Charlie," Mia said, darting away in a fit of

laughter before he could catch her.

"That was a good one. Congratulations."

"I thought it was pretty funny," Celeste said with a smirk. She led them onto the sand, right past the perimeter of the gym. That close, a dank musk hung in the air, the combination of heavy cologne and sweat. One of the weight lifters noticed Celeste and whistled as she walked past, igniting an onslaught of catcalls from the other musclemen.

She didn't turn her head or act like she heard them but Charlie saw the smile creep onto her face and read her look of satisfaction. It was clear that he and his sisters weren't enough—Celeste needed the whole world to notice her.

"What about here?" Without waiting for a response, Celeste dropped her bag and kicked off her shoes at one of the only empty spots next to the beach volleyball courts, where four games were in progress. A bunch of kids were camped out all around the courts, tanning and cheering on their friends.

Charlie stood, still holding his towel. With the tide low, the beach stretched on for hundreds of feet beyond them, much of it empty. "What about closer to the ocean?"

"It's more fun here," Celeste said, laying out her towel in full view of the main court, where four shirtless guys were engaged in a heated game of two-on-two.

Charlie ignored her and started heading down toward the water. The voices on the boardwalk gradually gave way to the sound of crashing waves and seagulls flying overhead. He took off his shirt and dropped his towel on a section of hard-packed sand not far from the lifeguard shack and ran the rest of the way down to the ocean. He went in up to his knees and stared

out at the expansive horizon, seaweed lapping around his legs as the waves receded around him.

"This is as far as I go." Celeste had followed him down and was standing a few feet behind, right at the water's edge. "Do you realize how polluted this water is?"

"I'm glad I could tear you away from the game," Charlie said, coming out of the water.

"In case you haven't noticed, I'm not the only one they idolize."

He looked back toward the beach, where his sisters were laying out their towels on either side of his. He was surprised, not so much that they felt that way about him but that Celeste was the one to remind him.

He went up to join them. They spent the next hour building a massive sand castle, while Celeste lay out in the sun. Despite all the shopping and the tattoos and the fascination with Celeste, he was relieved to discover that his sisters were still just eleven-year-old girls.

"Can we get some ice cream?" Heather asked, spotting a man selling it from a cart farther down the beach.

"Want some?" he asked Celeste.

She shook her head no. Charlie pulled a ten-dollar bill out of his wallet and handed it to Heather. "You go with her," he told Mia. "And I'll have . . . Rocky Road. If they don't have it, just vanilla."

Charlie adjusted his towel so he could see them as they went.

"That's weird," Celeste said, pulling her towel next to his. "Those are Molly's favorite flavors."

Charlie stiffened. In all this time, they had never talked about Molly. He wasn't sure what Celeste did or didn't know about their relationship, but he erred on the side of caution and assumed it wasn't much. After

all, she hadn't mentioned Molly in so long. Maybe Molly really was that private—so private, she didn't even share things with her best friend. For some reason Charlie preferred it this way, keeping things separate. It was almost as if whatever was happening with Molly existed in its own universe, where regular life didn't get in the way. "Not surprising. They're only two of the most popular flavors in the world," he covered.

"You should even out that farmer's tan of yours," Celeste said, lying back down on her towel. "Don't worry. I can see the girls from here."

Charlie looked at the contrasting colors of his skin. She was right. His arms, all the way up to his biceps, were a rich, golden brown, while the rest of his torso and shoulders were pasty white from the countless hours he spent on the trails.

He leaned back and lay down next to her. He could see the curves of her body from the corner of his eye, the way her chest heaved up and down with each breath. She was wearing the same pink bikini she'd had on that day at her father's house.

"Doesn't this feel great?"

Great? No. It felt confusing. Completely confusing. He was totally attracted to Celeste, like, physically. But it was Molly he went to sleep and woke up thinking about. She was the one he wanted to share things with, wanted to know better. Why?

He concentrated on the sun's hot rays beating down on him, warming his entire body. "Yeah, it's nice."

"See? I know how to appreciate the simple things in life."

A few minutes later, Charlie glanced over at Celeste. She had fallen asleep and now her leg was leaning against his. She looked so peaceful with her eyes closed, with the small sun freckles dotting her nose and forehead. He

wondered why she couldn't always be like this, so calm and natural.

He left her leg there until he saw his sisters walking toward them, their hands full of ice cream.

• • •

Snowpeak99: there u are.

Snowpeak99: been waiting for u all night.

Snowpeak99: cheese is here too. he says hello.

Snowpeak99: molly? r u there?

Mollypop: yeah.

Snowpeak99: did you have a good night?

Mollypop: yup.

Snowpeak99: that's good.

Snowpeak99: is everything ok?

Mollypop: why?

Snowpeak99: just asking.

Snowpeak99: u don't seem yourself.

Mollypop: i'm fine.

Snowpeak99: okay.

Snowpeak99: but if there's anything u want to talk about . . .

Mollypop: how many girlfriends have u had?

Snowpeak99: what do u mean?

Mollypop: just forget it.

Snowpeak99: i don't want to forget it.

Snowpeak99: i'm gonna answer you.

Snowpeak99: i'm just wondering where this is coming from.

Snowpeak99: cuz you seem mad at me or something.

Mollypop: i'm not mad at you.

Mollypop: i'm mad at myself.

Snowpeak99: can u explain what's going on?

Mollypop: i let you convince me you were different.

Snowpeak99: what? molly, you have to tell me what you're talking about.

Mollypop: i saw those pictures of you with all your girlfriends.

Snowpeak99: the ones in the drawer?

Mollypop: yes.

Snowpeak99: ok, so, i'm going to ignore the fact that you went through my locked drawer for now.

Snowpeak99: i know how it must look, but you have to believe i'm not like that.

Mollypop: it doesn't matter anyway.

Snowpeak99: it does matter. it matters a lot. i want to explain. Because i think i finally figured it out.

Snowpeak99: for whatever reason, i have an easy time meeting people but it never turns into anything real.

Snowpeak99: because i've never met a girl i can relate to.

Snowpeak99: except for you.

Snowpeak99: u have no reason to believe me, i know.

Snowpeak99: but i really like you, molly.

Snowpeak99: a lot.

Snowpeak99: r u still with me?

Mollypop: yeah, i'm here.

Snowpeak99: i mean it, molly.

Snowpeak99: it's different with you.

Snowpeak99: you have to trust that and judge me by my actions.

Snowpeak99: not by my past.

Mollypop: ok . . . i'll try.

With one breath, with one flow / You will know . . .

—The Police, "Synchronicity I"

She consulted the map a third time before leaving the main trail. The path wasn't much wider than her bike and was easy to miss, but the turnoff was next to a small patch of yellow wildflowers, just like Charlie had told her it would be. She had practically memorized his e-mail, and it ran through her head as she braved the terrain of thorny bushes, scattered rocks, and branches.

Charlie hadn't told Molly where she was going, but he had gone to the trouble of hand-drawing a map, scanning it into the computer, and sending it off with the e-mail that had been waiting for her when she woke up. He even drew in details like the cluster of flowers by the turnoff and a tree stump she would be passing farther down the trail. The only vague part of the map was the destination. The trail zigzagged its way around the mountain, ending at a spot marked with an *X*.

You'll know you're there when you see it. Leave the bike and walk through the opening. Lie down and listen to the song I've attached. Besides me, you're now the only person in the world who knows about this place. Keep it sacred.

She pushed her way through the thicket. Two months ago she would never have believed she would be up and out this early on a bike, trusting some guy she'd never met, riding blindly toward who knew what. But this was the closest they'd come to being on a date, out in the world. Even though they were hundreds of miles apart, this ride was still something that only they would ever experience, together or apart.

There wasn't a chance in the world that she was going to miss out on it.

I've been thinking about you all night. He had really written that. To her. She needed to keep repeating it to herself, over and over like a mantra. They were the words she had longed to hear from someone, anyone. She didn't know what she had done to deserve it now, but it felt good. Good enough to get scratched up and down her legs—good enough to keep going, destination unknown.

I've been thinking about you all night.

The truth was, she couldn't stop thinking about him either.

After a few near falls, Molly was finally convinced that the path was so narrow and the bushes so thick on either side that they would cushion her if she really was going to take a major spill. She released the brakes and let the hill carry her along until it leveled out into a forest of pines. She wove her way around the trees, breathing in their fresh, stimulating scent, until she reached the other side of the mountain and rode out onto a clearing in front of a large cluster of rocks. A few hundred feet beyond, the hill dipped back down into a canyon of stone and trees.

Walk through the opening.

She crouched down and stepped through the makeshift entrance created by the overlapping boulders.

You'll know you're there.

She kneeled lower and crawled the rest of the way in on top of a layer

of pine needles. Charlie had clearly gathered them from the surrounding trees and laid them out like a carpet. She looked around at this secret cave, perched on the edge of the forest on top of the mountain. It felt surreal and beautiful and otherworldly. Like a place in a fairy tale.

She took out her iPod, put on her headphones, and lay down on the bed of needles, staring up at the canopy of stone overhead. The upbeat melody of "Such Great Heights", by The Postal Service started to play. She closed her eyes and listened.

They will see us waving from such great
Heights, "Come down now," they'll say
But everything looks perfect from far away

It felt like Charlie was speaking directly to her through the song, like they were his lyrics specially meant for her. Molly lay there listening until she eventually dozed off.

• • •

When she woke up, the sun had risen so high that shafts of light darted all around her, creeping through the openings above. She could now see the mossy green hue of the surrounding rocks and a single purple wildflower poking up from the damp earth by the entrance. She poked her head outside the cave, where the distorted shadow of a bird glided in and out of existence. One second Molly could make out the contours of a wing, the next it was gone.

A few minutes later the actual bird appeared, hovering above, revealing its red underbelly and the bright yellow, blue, and green of the rest of its feathers. She had never seen anything like it.

She watched it arc back and forth above her, stretching its wings wide

like it owned the sky.

She sat up with a start and fished her notebook out of her bag. She took another look at the bird and began to sketch.

• • •

It was almost five when she got to the store. She hadn't checked in or told Penelope she was taking the day off, because she hadn't known herself until the day just happened. Penelope would be closing any minute, but that wasn't why she was there.

"Oh my! What happened to you?" Penelope asked, taking in Molly's state.

She had gone straight there from the trail, with cuts and mud all over her legs and pine needles stuck in her hair, still wearing Charlie's yellow COLORADO T-shirt. She walked with purpose down the center of the store toward Penelope, who was sitting behind the desk. Molly pulled up her usual chair, reached into her bag, and handed Penelope her sketchbook. "I want you to see this."

She leaned back and closed her eyes as Penelope flipped through the pages.

"These are fabulous," she said when she was done. "You have to do something with these."

"I know," Molly said. "And I need your help."

• • •

Charlie vaguely heard a persistent honking outside and pulled the pillow over his head to block it out. He was exhausted from having been up practically all night the night before, and was trying to crash early.

The honking stopped and was replaced with the sharp staccato of a handful of pebbles hitting the window almost simultaneously.

He shot out of bed and looked outside.

"What are you doing?" he cried. Celeste was leaning against her father's red Porsche, still idling in the middle of the road. It sparkled, even in the dark.

"Come on down and you'll find out."

She was being the same old Celeste, trying to playfully lure him toward her with her L.A.-cool facade. He doubted she had gone to all the trouble of getting the Porsche for her own benefit.

"Give me two minutes," he told her.

• • •

Charlie had learned to drive a stick, but it took a couple of blocks until he felt comfortable behind the wheel. The car had so much force, he barely had to touch the gas pedal to make it take off.

"Looks like you're ready. Take a left here."

Charlie didn't ask any questions, just followed Celeste's instructions as she directed him up a steep, windy road.

"Right! Right, right now!"

"How about a little notice!" Charlie made the sudden turn, not expecting it to be so sharp, but the car complied, sturdily hugging the road around the corner. He kept driving uphill, following the snaky route he was now accustomed to in L.A. from having ridden his bike everywhere, until it ended at a large black gate. It was the entrance to a path in the Hollywood Hills. It was, in fact, *the* path that led to the Hollywood sign. Even in the dark Charlie could see the iconic white letters perched at the top of the hill.

"What are we doing here? It's locked."

The headlights revealed the thick chain around the gate and a sign that read CLOSED. NO ACCESS TO HOLLYWOOD SIGN.

Celeste hopped out in front of the car without answering. Fully illuminated,

she took out a key, placed it in the padlock, and next thing he knew, she was pushing the gate open and motioning for Charlie to drive in.

"How do you even have that key?" Charlie asked when she got back in the car.

"One of the perks of my dad being a slimeball producer. He shot a movie here last year, and *someone* conveniently made copies of his keys." She pressed a button and all the windows rolled down. "Don't just sit there, let's go!"

Charlie shifted into first, released the clutch, and pressed the gas. It was pitch-black in the canyon, with only the moon and light from the occasional house spotting the outskirts of the hills. But the headlights brightened the path enough to convince him that they weren't going to drive off into the dark abyss. He shifted into second and then third.

"That's more like it," Celeste yelled over the rumbling engine.

Now that he was used to the car, he felt more confident picking up the pace and pressed his foot down even further, the speedometer nearing forty. He slowed down as the road suddenly veered left, ending a few hundred feet ahead at a fence, behind which stood what looked like a radio transmission tower. Charlie got out of the car, leaving the headlights on.

"What is this place?" It looked empty and creepy, like an abandoned research post in some sci-fi movie.

"I have no idea," Celeste said, walking in the other direction. "But that's not why we're here."

He followed her down the road to an opening in the fence, behind which stood the nine letters of the Hollywood sign.

Celeste crouched down and slipped through the tear, barely managing to avoid snagging her dress on the fence.

"You're nuts," Charlie said, squeezing through next.

He wasn't expecting the hill to be so steep. He grabbed onto a tangle of tree roots for balance as he made his way down, sideways.

"Hoist me up." She was standing behind an *O*, her hands gripping the bottom of the letter, waiting for Charlie to help push her up the rest of the way, into its center.

He formed a step with his hands and launched her up. He was both tall and strong enough to lift himself up next.

"Isn't this awesome?" Celeste asked. They were squeezed in with their legs dangling over the edge like a swing, the curve of the *O* pushing them each in toward the middle.

It *was* incredible. Charlie felt like he was floating over the city. "So what am I, the hundredth guy you've brought up here?"

Celeste got quiet and looked away. "Actually, you're the first."

It was not the answer he'd expected, but he believed her. They were now sitting so close that her hair gently brushed against his cheek. It smelled sweet, like cucumber.

They turned toward each other at the same time.

Look away, Charlie, he told himself. *Look away.*

The wind blew her hair into her eyes. Charlie reached over to push it away, letting his hand linger on her cheek.

Celeste inched her face closer, her eyes locked on his, when the choppy drone of a helicopter interrupted. Less than a minute later, it flew right over them, briefly revealing their position with its roaming searchlight.

"Run!" Celeste laughed.

She slid down to the ground and sprinted back up the hill, with Charlie right behind. They got in the car and rolled most of the way down, with the engine and headlights off to avoid detection.

They didn't speak much the rest of the way home, aware of what had almost happened. Both things.

Celeste muttered something about the stupid helicopter ruining their good time, but Charlie was relieved it had.

He wasn't so sure he could have pulled away on his own.

From: Molly
To: Charlie
Date: July 17, 2008 10:58 P.M. MST
Subject: such great heights

C,

It's the most magical place in the world!!!! I'm sooo honored you shared it with me. I felt like I was in the middle of nowhere and totally lost track of time. I just lay there all day sketching. I had so many ideas I could barely draw them fast enough—I didn't even realize so much time had passed. it was like I was transported or something. Crazy!!! Has that ever happened to you?

Anyway, IM as soon as you can. I have so much more to tell you!!!

xoxoxoxox
M

Charlie's insides tightened. He felt like such a jerk, like he had betrayed Molly, even though nothing had happened. If Molly had sent the e-mail just a few minutes earlier, he never would have gone out with Celeste. He also knew he couldn't continue this way. Something had to give.

He hit reply.

From: Charlie
To: Molly
Date: July 17, 2008 11:01 P.M. PST
Subject: Re: such great heights

___

M,

I'm so glad you loved it. I had a feeling you would. I'll be up for a while if you get this tonight. I have something I want to talk about with you too.

C

. . .

Mollypop: boo.

Mollypop: u still awake?

Snowpeak99: hey. i thought u were down for the count.

Mollypop: nope . . . WIDE awake . . . too excited to sleep!

Mollypop: so what did u want to tell me?

Snowpeak99: you go first.

Mollypop: it's been THE best day.

Mollypop: that cave was the most special place i've ever been.

Mollypop: i'm so so honored you shared it with me.

Snowpeak99: so no trouble finding it?

Mollypop: nope, not at all.

Mollypop: your map was perfect.

Mollypop: i fell asleep for a while on top of all those pine needles—so comfy, who knew?!

Mollypop: when i woke up there was this amazing bird flying back and forth right out front.

Mollypop: i've never seen one like it.

Snowpeak99: what'd it look like?

Mollypop: it was so beautiful . . . like a red robin.

Mollypop: but only its stomach was red. he had a blue head and a green back. . . . it was the coolest thing.

Snowpeak99: no way. sounds like you saw a painted bunting.

Mollypop: of course you knew what it was! have you ever seen one?

Snowpeak99: just once.

Snowpeak99: they're incredibly rare in colorado.

Mollypop: really? well . . . it was definitely rare to me! this leads to my other news. . . .

Mollypop: after seeing the bird I suddenly got a design idea.

Mollypop: and i literally just sat there for hours sketching.

Mollypop: I didn't even realize how late it was when i finished.

Snowpeak99: that's SO great.

Mollypop: there's more.

Mollypop: i've decided to go for the internship.

Mollypop: i talked to penelope about it and everything.

Snowpeak99: AWESOME.

Mollypop: she's going to help me so i can get it done in time.

Mollypop: i'm so excited!!! i know i keep saying that but it's true.

Mollypop: and it's all because of you.

Snowpeak99: i have to see you, molly.

Mollypop: what do u mean?

Snowpeak99: i don't think i can wait till the end of the summer.

Snowpeak99: i really want to meet u in person and i figured out a way.

Mollypop: r u serious?

Snowpeak99: completely.

Mollypop: how?

Snowpeak99: i'm going to utah for a weekend to visit my friend dan.

Snowpeak99: his uncle lives in park city and we go every summer.

Snowpeak99: it's a big house with lots of room.

Snowpeak99: i looked it up and it's almost exactly halfway between boulder and L.A.

Snowpeak99: so what i'm saying is . . .

Snowpeak99: i really want you to come.

Snowpeak99: and meet me there for the weekend.

Snowpeak99: if you think you could get away.

Snowpeak99: but i don't want to pressure you or anything.

Mollypop: wow.

Snowpeak99: is that a good wow?

Mollypop: when r u going?

Snowpeak99: august 1.

Snowpeak99: u don't have to answer me now.

Mollypop: that's in two weeks . . . the day i hand in my application.

Snowpeak99: even more reason to celebrate.

Snowpeak99: it might seem crazy but I just really want to see you.

Mollypop: tell me how to get there.

I'm adding something new to the mixture / So there's a different hue to your picture / A different ending to this fairy tale . . .

—The Raconteurs, "Together"

Molly burrowed under the blanket, where she came face-to-face with Yoda, the Jedi Master. She had dug Charlie's *Star Wars* sheets out from the bottom of the laundry basket and put them back on the bed before going to sleep. They smelled just like his yellow T-shirt. Her spine tingled as she wrapped the sheets around her. In less than two weeks, Charlie's arms would be enveloping her.

In less than two weeks. It was real. It was happening. They had stayed up practically all night planning the trip, down to coordinating their arrival in Salt Lake City within an hour of each other. But there was so much to accomplish before Molly could even contemplate getting on that bus.

If she didn't get started, she would never make it.

She sat up with a start when she heard the sound of an incoming instant message. She had fallen asleep next to her open laptop, which was becoming a habit.

DoctoRina: I'M HOME!!!!!

Mollypop: oh, reen! i'm so relieved. . . . even though i still don't get to see you, it feels better knowing that you're back on this continent.

DoctoRina: so what's the latest? i've spent the last month stuck with my grandparents and fifty thousand relatives so i need gossip.

Mollypop: you're never going to believe what's happened.

DoctoRina: tell me!!!! i'm dying over here. . . .

Mollypop: there's so much, i don't even know where to start. . . . first, i'm applying for the internship! i'm so excited, reen. i'm really doing it and i'm going to work my butt off for the next two weeks. penelope said she's going to help and write my letter and everything.

DoctoRina: GREAT, molls! you're totally going to win too. i can feel it.

Mollypop: there's more. charlie asked me to meet him in utah for the weekend after i hand in my application.

DoctoRina: NO. WAY.

Mollypop: i know . . . it's so crazy i kind of can't believe it either.

DoctoRina: your mom was cool with it?

Mollypop: she doesn't exactly know, and i kinda want to leave it that way.

DoctoRina: how???

Mollypop: well . . . i was hoping that maybe i could say i was with you and your family?

DoctoRina: in utah??!!

Mollypop: she'd never find out or have any reason to not believe me. . . . i'm not psyched about lying to her, but i really can't risk her saying no.

Mollypop: i can't explain how much this trip means to me.

Mollypop: so please, please, please could you do this one favor for me?

DoctoRina: on one condition.

Mollypop: okay . . .

DoctoRina: i have to meet him first.

DoctoRina: it's not that i don't trust you, please know that, but i'm the only person in the world who's gonna know where you really are, so it'd make me feel better if you let me at least talk to the guy first.

Mollypop: that seems fair . . . but please at least pretend you're picking something up for me so he doesn't think i'm spying on him or anything??

DoctoRina: like what?

Mollypop: how about the silver thimble in my sewing basket?

DoctoRina: the one i gave you?

Mollypop: yup! :)

Mollypop: and reen?

DoctoRina: yeah?

Mollypop: please like him!

DoctoRina: if you do, i'm sure he's great.

● ● ●

Molly arrived at the store an hour early so she could get right to work on her application. The designs she'd sketched in the cave had come out so well that now she just had to narrow them down to her top five for her portfolio. From that group, she'd select her favorite to make as the prototype for her collection. She took out her key to unlock the shop's door, but it was already open.

It was dark inside, except for a glow coming from the back room. "Hello?" she called out.

Penelope emerged a minute later with a broom and cloth in hand.

"What are you doing here so early?" Molly asked, relieved that it was Penelope and not some burglar.

"There you are. Just in time. Come here, I want to show you something."

Molly followed Penelope into the storage room and stood, mouth agape, at the door. It was unrecognizable. All the boxes had been unpacked and cleared out. The once cluttered shelves had been tidied and lined with vintage accessories from costume jewelry to handbags. But best of all, a large drafting table had appeared and now sat in the center of the room with a sewing machine placed on top. "I can't believe all this. Penelope, it's . . . I don't even know what to say."

"Well, good, because there's no time to chat. We need to get going. I made a list of all the fabric stores in the area. If you don't find anything there, we can close early and head into Denver. They have a much bigger selection."

"Thanks, but I kind of was hoping I could use something from here and, you know, recycle the fabric."

"Honey, you can use anything in this store—whether it's for sale or hanging off my back—but are you sure you don't want to pick exactly what you had in mind?"

"This *is* what I had in mind. There are so many beautiful things here right in front of us." She took a white cotton eyelet dress off the rack and held it up. "I mean, look at this. I could dye the fabric and use it to ruffle the collar. Oh, and I decided which dress I want to make." She walked over to the table and opened the sketchbook to the correct page. "It's this one here."

Penelope looked at the design and smiled. "It's perfect."

In all the world there is no heart for me like yours. In all the world, there is no love for you like mine.

—Maya Angelou

"Guess who I'm going to see, little guy," Charlie said, rubbing Cheese's chin. "That's right, your favorite person!"

He'd double-checked the Greyhound schedule from both L.A. and Boulder to Salt Lake City and then bought their tickets online. He made sure his bus got in first so he could get Molly flowers and scope out a place to eat when she arrived. They were going to have an hour together before catching the bus to Park City, and he wanted to make sure they could spend it somewhere nice. It was weird to think that in twelve days he'd be sitting right in front of her, face-to-face. He'd finally be able to touch her smooth, pale skin and see her dark, mysterious eyes up close.

"Charlieeeee! There's someone here to see you," Heather screamed from downstairs.

Charlie turned to look at Cheese, who was sitting on the pillow next to him. He still hadn't left the room or gotten out of bed, and it was almost

noon. "Who could it be, gray man?"

He threw on a pair of sweats and had a shirt halfway over his head on his way out the door when he ran smack into someone standing on the other side. "Oh, man, are you okay? I didn't see you."

"I'm sorry, your sister told me to come up. I was about to knock."

He pulled the shirt all the way on and saw who it was. He recognized her immediately. "Wait, you're Rina, right?"

She nodded. "I suppose Molly told you I'd be dropping by."

"She didn't, but I've heard about you," he explained. "And you're all over the wall." He pointed toward Molly's collage.

"Right, the wall. Oh, hey, Cheese." Rina ran over to pick him up, but he darted away and took refuge behind Charlie's legs. Rina tilted her head and squinted at Charlie. If he hadn't known better, he'd have thought she was sizing him up. "Wow, he likes you."

Charlie shrugged. "So did Molly send you to vouch for me?"

She looked up, busted. "Actually, it was my idea. I kind of insisted on it."

He smiled and sat down on the bed. "Well, ask me anything you want."

Rina blushed. "This seems so awkward now."

"Don't worry—I get it. I'm glad Molly has someone like you, looking out for her and everything."

Rina paused. "Are you for real and do you have a brother?"

Charlie laughed. "I'm not as great as I seem, but I guess I shouldn't be telling you that."

"Now I see why you two get along so well. You both have that modesty thing down to a tee."

"So, do you have any tips for me? For when we meet?"

"I don't think you need my help." She looked around the room and suddenly remembered Molly's request. "Oops, I almost forgot, Molly actually did want me to get something for her." She pulled the sewing basket out from under the desk and rummaged through until she found it. "Her lucky thimble."

"Her lucky thimble?" Charlie repeated, laughing.

"That's Molls. She has her quirks," Rina said, sliding the basket back under the desk. "Well, it was great meeting you—"

"Rina? Is that you?" Celeste sauntered into the room and tossed her bag on the bed before coming over to hug Rina. "When did you get back?"

"Last night. I'm so incredibly jet-lagged. I was in India," she explained to Charlie.

He shifted uncomfortably on his feet. "Oh, cool."

"What are you doing here?" Rina asked.

Charlie braced himself for Celeste's response, hoping she wouldn't say anything that Rina would misinterpret and relay back to Molly.

Celeste pointed at the closet. "Borrowing a Molly special for an event tonight." She sat on the edge of the bed. "What about you?"

"Picking this up for Molly," Rina said, holding out the thimble.

"Awesome," Celeste said. "That hopefully means she's making something new I can borrow!"

While Celeste was perusing Molly's wardrobe, Charlie walked Rina to the door. When he got back to his room, Celeste was standing half-naked, wearing only a black lace bra and matching underwear. "Um . . . what are you doing?"

"It's nothing you don't want to see." She caught his eye in the mirror's reflection.

"Put some clothes on," he said, turning away.

"What's *your* problem today?" She put her shirt back on. "You can turn around now."

"It's nothing," Charlie snapped. "I'm just busy."

"Yeah, I can see that," Celeste said smugly. "Don't worry, I'm really not here to see you." She went into the closet and came out thirty seconds later carrying five dresses. "See? All done. I'll get out of your way now."

Normally he would have apologized for being so harsh, but he couldn't. It wasn't Celeste he didn't trust so much as himself.

She stormed past him, scooping up her bag, and slammed the door on her way out.

• • •

From: Rina
To: Molly
Date: July 20, 2008 2:50 P.M. PST
Subject: OMG

Suffice it to say you have my blessing.

And I got your thimble.

P.S. Celeste is still raiding your closet, but I guess that's no surprise.

oxoxoxoxoxoxoxoxoxoxo RD

• • •

From: Charlie
To: Molly
Date: July 25, 2008 9:47 A.M. PST
Subject: Countdown

Only seven more days (sounds sooner than a week, don't you think?)

Was just thinking about you and wanted to let you know.

Going for a ride.

C

From: Molly
To: Charlie
Date: July 25, 2008 2:16 P.M. MST
Subject: Re: Countdown

You're the sweetest person in the world, Charlie Richards. Now it's only six and a half days away. That sounds even sooner.

On my way to the button store. Pray to the button gods that they have four matching gold buttons!

M

From: Charlie
To: Molly
Date: July 25, 2008 5:36 P.M. PST
Subject: buttons

I spent the last three hours praying to the button gods (there are four of them, it turns out). Did it work?

From: Molly
To: Charlie
Date: July 25,2008 8:18 P.M. MST
Subject: Re: buttons

It did! I found them at the first store. You're officially my hero now.

I love you without knowing how, or when, or from where.

—Pablo Neruda, "Love Sonnet XVII"

"Honey, there's someone named Charlie on the phone for you," Laura said, turning the volume down on the stereo.

Molly was listening to the music Charlie had sent her while hurrying to finish her application essay. Ron had offered to read it over, and she wanted to give it to him before he went to sleep. "Did you say Charlie?"

Laura nodded. "Who is he?"

Molly shot up, past her mother, downstairs to the receiver waiting off the hook on the side table in the hallway. "Hello?"

"Molly? Is that you?" the voice on the other end asked. It was deeper than she'd imagined.

"Hi, it's me." Her voice caught, like she had just woken up and was speaking for the first time that day.

"Wow. It's so great to hear your voice."

She switched the receiver to her other ear and tried to calm her trembling hands. "Yours too."

"I thought I'd call to wish you luck for tomorrow. I mean, it's such a big deal, so an e-mail didn't seem to cut it, you know?"

She was too nervous to respond.

"Also, I figured we should get our first awkward conversation out of the way before we meet."

Molly laughed. "Good thinking," she said, relieved that it wasn't just her. She started to breathe normally and relaxed her shoulders, which had been hiked up to her ears.

"So, is it going to be an all-nighter?"

"Shockingly, it's not. I mean, I have a zillion things to do tomorrow, but FedEx is open till, like, nine, so I'll have enough time."

"Molly?"

"Yeah?"

"I can't wait to see you."

She shuddered, hearing the sincerity and meaning in his voice. She couldn't imagine what seeing him was going to do to her.

"Molls, are you still there?" he asked tenderly.

"I'm here," she whispered back.

"Everything's going to be great."

She had every reason to believe he was right. She was about to submit her best work yet, something she could really be proud of, and in less than forty-eight hours she was going to meet the best guy she had ever known.

"I hope so."

"You should get some sleep," he said. "You have a big day tomorrow."

"Wait, Charlie, don't hang up!" she blurted before she could stop herself.

"What is it?"

Now that she had his undivided attention, the silence on the other end of the line was too intimidating. She couldn't be the first to say those three short words that dangled from the tip of her tongue. "I—I can't wait to see you either."

18

The way to love anything is to realize that it might be lost.

-- G.K. Chesterton

Ron was already sitting at the kitchen table when Molly came down for breakfast, her essay lying next to his plate with a half-eaten bagel on it.

"You're up early," he said, taking a sip of his coffee.

"I'm too excited to sleep." She poured herself a glass of orange juice and sat down next to him.

"I read your essay," he said, putting down his cup. "And I wouldn't change a single word."

"You really think so?" Molly was nervous because she hadn't presented any facts or addressed the business aspect of the industry, which was a big part of what the internship was about. She'd decided to just write about what she knew best: why fashion mattered to her. She really believed that more than just making pretty clothes, a designer had the opportunity to help people express different parts of their personalities through style. That's why each piece in her collection was so diverse, to account for the whole person and how we aren't necessarily the same every day.

Ron reached his arm around her shoulders. "I hope that you know I'm proud of you."

It was the first time his touch didn't make her squirm. "If you don't have anything to do," she said, "I was going for a quick ride before heading to the store."

"Really? I would love that," Ron said, getting up from his chair. "Give me two minutes to change."

• • •

Molly led the way along the city streets to the Betasso Preserve. She had been riding the three-mile trail every morning for the last two weeks before going in to work on her application.

"It's basically a loop," Molly explained when they got to the trail entrance. "It gets a little steep at points, but then it'll even out."

"Got it."

They made their way up, mostly in tandem with Molly in the lead, riding side by side when they could in the grassy meadows. They fell into a quiet, comfortable rhythm, like they had done this together a million times before.

"Three hundred yards to the finish line," Molly called out, pulling ahead for the final stretch.

"I let you win," Ron said amid deep, panting breaths when he reached the gate a few paces behind.

"I bet you were faster when you were my age," she said, riding circ around him while he sprayed water over his face.

Molly threw her head back and stared up at the clear blue sky. "Qui Look up!" she suddenly said, pointing above.

Ron followed the direction of her finger to a bright, colorful bird, flying overhead. "Wow. I've never seen a bird like that."

"It's a painted bunting. I saw one just the other day."

They watched the bird's meandering path, a red, blue, and green paintball floating across the sky. Molly was certain that nothing in her world had ever looked so beautiful.

• • •

Molly rode straight to the store from the trail, thinking about Charlie the whole way. The painted bunting was a sign. She was convinced of it. A sign that her life was going to turn out all right, much better than she had ever expected.

This time tomorrow I'll be on my way to see him.

She kept imagining her arrival, how Charlie would be waiting for her when she got off the bus. She wondered when they would first kiss, whether it would be right away, or later that night, after they'd had time to get used to each other. But one thing was certain—there *would* be a kiss. Her whole body fluttered just thinking about it.

The front door was locked and the sign in the front window said CLOSED even though all the lights were on and Molly could see Penelope inside through the window. "What's going on?" she asked, wheeling her bike to the back.

"We're closed today," Penelope said.

"I see that, but why?"

"I figured you could use an extra pair of hands, and our customers can wait. I don't want any argument out of you," she said, as Molly was about to open her mouth.

"Penelope! Thank—"

"You can thank me later. Let's get to work."

In the last two weeks the back room had become a full working studio. Scraps of cut fabric were spread out across the long, wide table next to the sewing machine. Molly's sketches were tacked to a bulletin board hanging on the wall behind her workbench. Unlike the magazine cutouts she had up in her bedroom at home, which were almost exclusively from *Vogue*, most of these were nature shots of things like pine trees, wildflowers, and mountain peaks—all the things she had come to appreciate on her trail rides. She had even found a picture of a painted bunting on the Internet that she'd enlarged and color printed on glossy paper at Kinko's. It hung in the middle of the board so she could look directly at it while she was at the sewing machine.

She had touched up and redrawn her sketches to make them more presentable, and arranged them in a folder, with a guide describing the intended color and fabric of each item.

All she had left to do was review all her materials and make the final adjustments to the dress, her prototype.

She got goose bumps looking at it, even still on the dress form. The color had turned out exactly the way she had envisioned. It was a yellow cotton ruffle-trimmed dress with cap sleeves made from a combination of items she'd repurposed and dyed the same color, with round gold buttons down the center.

"Aren't you going to try it on?" Penelope asked, snapping Molly out of her reverie. She had the pins ready to mark the spots for alteration.

Penelope helped her take it off the model. Molly held her breath as she carefully slipped it on over her head, pushing one arm through the sleeve, then the other, until it was hanging on her body. The ruffles fell perfectly and the sleeves hit at exactly the right angle, right above the bicep.

"Oh, Molly," Penelope said, cupping her hands over her mouth.

"Don't cry yet! The hem's too long."

"Okay, okay," Penelope said, crouching down to pin the bottom.

When she was done, Molly slipped out of the dress and shortened it on the sewing machine.

Her mother arrived in time to see Molly wearing the dress for the final fitting before she had to pack it up to ship.

"Don't move. You either, Penelope," Laura instructed, pointing a camera at them. "This is absolutely incredible, Molls. I just can't get over what you've done." She walked around the studio, taking in all the details that had gone into putting the dress and the entire portfolio together.

"Thanks, Mom." This was one compliment Molly could take. For the first time, she hadn't been afraid to let herself go and let her creativity take over, and it had led to the best work of her life so far.

"I'm so glad you have this special weekend planned with Rina. I want you to each get a mssage at the spa on me," she said, handing Molly two one-hundred-dollar bills.

Molly had never lied to her mother before—not about something as big as this. Laura might have agreed to let her go if she had explained everything, but Molly hadn't been able to take the chance of her saying no.

In the last couple of weeks things had started to return to normal between them, which made Molly feel even guiltier. "I don't think we're going to ave time for that," she said, trying to hand the money back.

"Then use it for something else," Laura insisted. "I'm sure you'll think something."

• • •

From: Molly

To: Charlie

Date: July 31, 2008 9:09 P.M. MST

Subject: Done!

I finished!!!!! My mom and Ron and Penelope surprised me after we went to FedEx with balloons and cake and champagne. It was so much fun, and I'm a tiny bit tipsy now from like half a glass (I know, lightweight), but don't worry, I plan on getting plenty of rest for tomorrow. . . . Off to pack!!

I really, really can't wait!!!!!

xoxo

Molls

• • •

It felt like it had been a long time since the whole family had had dinner together—his mothers' work schedules were a lot busier than either of them had anticipated—but everyone managed to make it home since Charlie was leaving for the weekend.

"Why don't you fly?" Lisa suggested, as she served out plates of hot apple pie. "It's such a long drive and it's not too late to book something."

"I really don't mind the bus. And it's easier since I'm bringing my bike. The offer was a sure sign they felt guilty for dragging him to L.A. for the summer since it hadn't panned out the way they expected, with family road trips and more free time. The irony was that, in spite of that, it was turning out to be the best summer of Charlie's life.

"I'll get it!" Mia and Heather said in unison when the doorbell rang. They raced to the door.

Charlie already knew it was Celeste from the way the twins greeted her with squeals and laughter. They always got that way around babysitters and older girls they looked up to.

Charlie hadn't seen Celeste since she stormed out of his room. He decided that it was just easier that way, especially now that he had made his choice.

"Celeste, what a nice surprise," Sally said, pulling up a chair. "Why don't you join us for some dessert?"

"Thanks but I just came by to borrow something from Molly's closet, if that's okay."

"Where you going?" Mia asked.

"I'm meeting some friends at the Farmers Market for karaoke night."

"Can we come? Please!!" Heather started the campaign, with Mia quickly joining in.

"Girls, come on, Celeste already has plans," Sally said, trying to quiet them.

"I'll take you guys there another time," Celeste offered. "But you can come if you want," she said nonchalantly, throwing a glance Charlie's way. It was the first time she had even acknowledged he was in the room.

Everyone stared, waiting for him to respond. Saying no would make him look like an ass, especially since he didn't have anything else to do. She was meeting friends, so it wouldn't be so bad, and he'd wanted to check out the market anyway since Molly had mentioned how much she loved it there.

The words came out of his mouth in a rush. "Sure, I'll go."

Celeste ran up to Molly's room to change and came down in a low-cut green and a short jean skirt that made her legs look like they went on forever.

"No Porsche tonight?" Charlie asked, getting in her SUV.

"Nope." She was still giving him the cold shoulder.

Charlie ignored her and looked out the window. She was baiting him, but he wasn't going to engage; he was going to stay strong.

They arrived at the open-air market a few minutes later and wove their way through the scents of the Greek, Chinese, and Cajun stalls blending together in an alluring way as they passed.

Charlie heard two girls doing a really bad, off-key rendition of "Livin' on a Prayer" as they approached the area where clusters of people were gathered around tables, in line for the bar, or on the makeshift dance floor in front of the mic where the karaoke machine was set up.

It didn't take long to figure out that (a) Celeste wasn't meeting any friends and (b) she was only there to drink.

"Wait right here." She forced her way to the front of the line, flashing a demure smile to the guys she pushed out of her way, ignoring the girls who protested, and got the bartender's attention in about ten seconds flat by leaning over the counter and flashing her cleavage.

She returned balancing a beer and two overflowing shot glasses.

"What is it?" Charlie asked, eyeing the pink concoction.

"I have no idea, but they were free." She downed her shot and chased it with some beer. "This one's for you, in case it wasn't clear," she said, waiting for him to drink.

He forced it down and took a swig of beer too, mainly to keep Celeste from drinking it all. She was the one driving, and he wanted to keep it that way, but it was too late. She was already on her way back to the bar for more.

She returned with two more shots, only this time they were blue. "Are

aking our way through the colors of the rainbow?" Charlie asked, taking
s.

"Shut up and drink."

She pounded the shot, grabbed his hand, and pulled him onto the
ance floor, squeezing their way to the middle, where they were packed
, surrounded on all sides by drunken dancers singing along to the music.
eleste started swaying her body, the same way she had at the party in the
lls, only this time she was inching toward Charlie. The combination of
e alcohol, which was just now starting to hit him, and the crowd made it
ifficult to move when she started rubbing up against him.

She leaned in close and whispered into his ear, "Are you going to admit
ou've been avoiding me?"

Her breath smelled like pink lemonade. "No." That was all he could
anage to say. Every fiber in him was telling him to run, but he couldn't,
nd instead he allowed her to run her fingers through his thick, wavy hair.

Everything happened pretty fast after that. One minute they were dancing
nd the next Celeste had her lips pressed against his.

"Let's get out of here," she whispered again, leading him off the dance
oor.

AUGUST

Have you thought about how this relationship will end?

—Judy Blume, *Forever* . . .

Molly was too excited to fall asleep. She stared up at the stars glowing on the ceiling. They now reminded her of so much more than just her dad.

She checked her e-mail again to see if there was a new message from Charlie. She still hadn't heard back from him all night. He'd never said he was going to respond, but it still seemed strange.

The old Molly would have been convinced it was a sign that Charlie suddenly didn't like her anymore and the whole thing was off, but the new Molly had no reason to believe that at all.

She shut her laptop, lay down, and closed her eyes, reminding herself that in less than twenty-four hours she and Charlie would be looking up at the real night sky together.

She didn't realize she had fallen asleep until the phone started ringing. She looked over at the clock; it was almost one.

It's Charlie, she thought. *Something is wrong.*

"Molls? You awake?" The door opened just wide enough for Laura's head to peek through.

Molly was already up and halfway to the door.

"It's Rina, honey. She was very insistent that she speak with you."

Molly ran past her and flew downstairs to the phone that was lying of the hook on the console in the hallway waiting for her.

"Rina? What's going on?" Molly hadn't actually spoken to Rina, hear her voice, in almost two months, and it wasn't the warmest way to greet he best friend, but her heart was pounding way too hard for niceties.

"Hi, Molls." Rina was trying to sound upbeat, as though she alway called in the middle of the night, but Molly could hear her voice catch an go up an octave. "I'm sorry to be calling so late. I tried your cell but—"

"I know, I don't get any reception," Molly jumped in, hoping to spee things along. "What's wrong, Reen? Just tell me."

"I hate to be doing this, but I felt you had to know." She paused befor continuing. "You can then decide what you want to do, and I swear I won pass any judgments."

Once she knew it wasn't Charlie calling, she hadn't considered that th bad news could possibly pertain to her. "Okay, okay, just tell me."

"I went to the Grove tonight to see a movie, and when I was walkin through the Farmers Market on my way to the car I saw Celeste."

"Uh-huh," Molly said. God! Couldn't Rina just spit it out?

"I was going to walk over and say hi but before I could she was . . . " Rina stopped to consider her choice of phrasing. "Well, she was kissin someone."

Molly stood frozen, listening. She knew where this was going, but she couldn get her mouth to form the words to tell Rina to stop, that she'd heard enough

"I don't really know how to tell you this, so I'm just going to say it. It as Charlie."

Molly slumped to the ground, still clutching the phone to her ear. She new it. She knew Rina was going to say exactly that. But hearing his name ut loud like that was even worse, because it meant that it was true.

"I'm so sorry, Molly."

She couldn't cry or move or speak.

"Molls? Are you still there?"

"I have to go," she whispered, letting go of the handset. It hung from ne table, spinning around in tight circles, months of coiled-up cord finally eing set free.

She could feel her mother's presence before she saw her. She closed her yes as she heard her approach.

"Let's get you upstairs." Laura wiped the hair out of Molly's face and, ith a hand on each of her shoulders, guided her up.

Can you make a mistake and miss your fate?

—Carrie Bradshaw, *Sex and the Ci*

Charlie started up when the alarm started blaring at five-fifteen in th morning.

"Turn it off," a voice grumbled above him.

He looked up from the floor, where he had spent the night, and sa Celeste in Molly's bed, coming to beneath a mountain of pillows. H stomach twisted into a thousand knots.

She's not supposed to be here.

"Whoa, scandal!" Celeste said, reading the mortification on Charli face. "It's more comfortable up here, you know."

He shot up and threw some clothes into a backpack and scanned t room for anything he might be missing. There was no way he was going let *this* make him miss his bus, which was leaving in less than an hour.

Now that he was more awake, the events of the night before started comi back. The only reason she was lying there was that she'd been too drunk go home, and having been too exhausted and tipsy himself, Charlie hadn't known what else to do with her, especially after she passed out in the cab on the way back. She had tried to convince him to let her drive home, but he'd refused, confiscating her keys, and hailed a taxi instead.

Nothing had happened beyond their initial kiss on the dance floor, but that was bad enough, and Charlie felt nauseous every time he thought about it.

"You have to go now." He was standing by the door, holding his backpack with his jacket on. He could barely look at her. "And, please," he said, finally making eye contact. "This stays between us."

• • •

The bus pulled into the Greyhound terminal thirty minutes late, but Charlie still had enough time to clean up a bit and get the flowers before Molly got there.

He went to the information booth first to make sure her bus was on time. A short, wide man wearing a burgundy vest and a name tag that read LARRY greeted him.

"How can I help you, sir?"

"I wanted to see if the bus from Boulder's on time?"

"That depends. When is it scheduled to arrive?" Larry asked in a very officious manner.

"It's due in at five."

Larry turned his attention to the computer screen. "Actually, it's coming in fifteen minutes early."

Charlie looked up at the clock in the middle of the terminal. "So you mean it'll be here in five minutes?"

"That's correct, sir. Gate twelve."

Charlie got a bottle of water, a pack of gum, and a bouquet of mixed flowers, then parked himself on a bench right in front of gate twelve. Every time he heard an engine approach he craned his neck to see if it was Molly's bus arriving. His head still hurt when he moved too suddenly, but much less than it had that morning. He'd had almost twelve hours to review the events of the night before and had decided that he was going to tell Molly what happened. And that meant *everything*. He didn't want any secrets between them, especially now that they were taking things to the next level; he was sure she'd understand.

The bus finally pulled in at four forty-five on the dot, just like Larry had said. Charlie rose from his seat and went to wait over by the entrance to the station, where he was visible but not in the way.

A depot worker appeared and opened the luggage compartment.

It felt like forever until a passenger, a middle-aged businessman who was decidedly not Molly, emerged.

A heavyset man was next, followed by a mother and her two sons.

An old woman got off next, but on her way down the steps she realized she had forgotten something, causing a delay in the exiting process.

"Hurry up," Charlie chastised the woman under his breath. The anxiety was killing him.

The woman reappeared a minute later, a steady stream of people disembarking behind her.

None of them were Molly, either.

Charlie stepped closer toward the bus. Maybe he'd be able to see her through the tinted windows, sitting in her seat, patiently waiting for her turn to get off.

But the bus seemed empty except for the driver, who was walking up and down the aisle, checking the seats and overhead bins to make sure nothing was left behind.

Something definitely was not right.

"This is the end of the road, son," the driver said, intercepting Charlie as he climbed the three steps onto the bus.

"Wait, my girlfriend's still on here." He didn't have time to think about his choice of words or that she wasn't technically his girlfriend. All he could focus on was the fact that Molly was nowhere in sight.

The driver followed Charlie down, shutting the door behind him. "Check the station. This bus is empty."

But Molly wasn't in the station, or the bathroom (he had three different women go in to check) or the parking lot or anywhere else in the vicinity.

He tried her cell continuously for almost an hour, getting voice mail each time. After leaving his tenth message, it finally began to sink in.

She wasn't coming.

21

All this time you were pretending / So much for my happy ending.

—Avril Lavigne, "My Happy Ending"

Molly had moved her stuff into Mia and Heather's room as soon as she woke up and hadn't left it all day.

She couldn't bear to be around Charlie's things or anything that reminded her of him, much less live in his room.

She had dragged all her belongings and dumped them in a messy, disorganized pile on one of the twin beds; she had spent most of the day sprawled out crying on the other.

Her mother and Ron had taken turns bringing her things like coffee and chocolate chip cookies to entice her out of her stupor.

But they didn't force her to talk. They just let her cry.

The phone rang at five forty-five in the afternoon. The shrill ring reverberated throughout the house. Molly knew it was Charlie. She'd been expecting his call.

Someone finally picked up after four long rings. Two minutes later, there was a knock at the door. It was like last night all over again, only this time it was Ron delivering the message.

"There's a boy named Charlie calling for you."

Even though she had been expecting this moment all day and had even prepared what she was going to say, just the sound of his name brought on another round of tears. She would not be marching downstairs the way she wished she could, picking up the phone and telling Charlie that she didn't have room for liars in her life and would appreciate it if he never contacted her again.

She wouldn't be making it beyond this room. "I can't . . . " she began. "I can't speak to him."

Ron gazed at her. Understanding, then steely resolve flashed in his eyes. "Don't worry, Molly. I'll take care of it."

• • •

There had to be some kind of explanation.

Charlie called the house and Ron answered after the fourth ring. He didn't introduce himself, but who else could it have been? Charlie asked to speak to Molly, the whole time hoping Ron would say, *Molly's away for the weekend*, and then she'd appear right next to him, ready to board the bus to Park City, the whole thing having been a big misunderstanding.

Instead, Ron said, "Let me see if she's available to come to the phone," and now Charlie was on hold waiting to speak to her.

He paced back and forth across the station, waiting for her to pick up, waiting to find out there was some simple explanation, some reason why she couldn't come or try to reach him.

"Hello? Are you still there?" It was still Ron, speaking in a harsher tone now.

"Yes, I'm here."

"Molly can't speak to you right now."

He said it with such finality. Like she wasn't just indisposed; she was deliberately avoiding him. "Okay, well—"

"Okay, then."

Ron was about to hang up when Charlie interrupted. "Wait. Can you please give her a message?"

There was a long pause.

"What is it?"

"Please tell her to call or e-mail as soon as she can. Whatever it is, I'll understand."

"Sure," he said. He didn't sound quite as gruff. "I can tell her that."

It was the final call for the bus to Park City but Charlie slid to the ground next to his bag. He felt like he'd been kicked in the gut and couldn't move. He sat there watching the world go by, feeling like he was no longer a part of it.

Nothing takes the taste out of peanut butter quite like unrequited love.

—Charlie Brown

"Charlie? Is that you?" Lisa emerged from the dark hallway just as Charlie was about to go upstairs.

"Hey. Change of plans."

"It's five o'clock in the morning. What happened?"

He was tired and confused and had been hoping to avoid seeing anyone for at least another few hours.

She turned on the light. "You look terrible. Come, I'll make you something to eat."

Charlie followed her into the kitchen and sat on a stool while she made the batter for pancakes. He hadn't eaten or slept all night, and could only obsessively think about Molly and what had gone wrong. There was no way she could have known about the incident with Celeste, since she should have already been on the bus by the time Charlie woke up. She had to have made up her mind to miss her bus before that, so there had to be something else to blame.

"This will make you feel better." Lisa handed him a cup of hot tea wit honey.

He felt a little more alert after a few sips. "Why are *you* awake?"

"Getting this paperwork out of the way so I can spend the day with th girls," she said, pointing to a pile of essays on the table.

After they finished eating, Lisa put her hand on top of his. "I'm concerne You still look awful."

Charlie laughed. "Thanks, Mom. I feel much better now."

Lisa smiled. "You know what I mean. Are you okay?"

Now that they were face-to-face, Charlie couldn't keep it in any longe He wasn't okay at all—he was completely heartbroken. He opened up an told her about Molly and their secret plan and why he'd done an about-fac when he got to Salt Lake City.

"Oh, Charlie," Lisa said, squeezing his hand. "That's so painful. Ther must be some kind of explanation."

It was a relief to talk about it, to get it off his chest after being alone for s many hours. "There's something else." If he was going to confide in her, h had to tell her everything. "Celeste kissed me last night, and I didn't exactl stop her. Not immediately anyway, like I should have. Once it happened, knew it was a mistake, and all I could think about was Molly."

Lisa sighed. "Is there any way she could have found out so fast?"

"I don't think so, but it doesn't matter. This is what I deserve for lettin it happen."

Lisa frowned. "If Molly really means that much to you, then you owe i to her and to yourself to find out what happened. Giving up because yo think you deserve it is the easy way out." She leaned over and kissed Charli on the forehead.

"Thanks, Mom."

Charlie helped Lisa clean up, then went up to Molly's room.

• • •

From: Charlie
To: Molly
Date: August 2, 2008 6:22 A.M. PST
Subject: Please call me

M,

I don't know what happened, and whatever it is, we can talk about it. I really hope you're okay and that nothing happened to you or anyone in your family.

I'm back in L.A. now. I turned right around when I heard you weren't coming. Anyway, please just let me know that you're okay.

I miss you.

C

I'll be the one who'll break my heart / I'll end it though you started it.

—Feist, "I Feel It All"

"Penelope! I'll see you tomorrow," Molly called. She walked toward Ron's car, which had just pulled up outside.

"All right, sweetie. It's good to have you back." Penelope caught up to her and gave her one of her trademark hugs.

It was Molly's first day back at the store in over a week, and Ron had offered to drive her in and pick her up. She couldn't contemplate getting on the bike; it reminded her too much of Charlie.

He had been calling the house every day, like clockwork, right before dinner—a time when he knew that Molly was usually home, just getting back from work. Ron took on the role of answering the phone, each time telling Charlie the same thing: that Molly was unavailable. She could only imagine how many e-mails were piled up in her inbox. Her laptop was another thing she was avoiding.

She got in the car and they rode along in silence, Molly slumped in her seat, staring out the window. She'd finally told her mother everything and had her fill Ron in—it was too painful to rehash the whole story from the beginning more than once. But Ron quietly assumed the role of a protective guardian, no questions asked, and was always there when the phone rang.

"The call already came today," he said, when they were almost at the house. She couldn't think of it as home anymore.

Her heart sank thinking about it, even though Ron was clearly trying to spare her the anticipation of waiting for the phone to ring when they got back. "That's a relief."

He didn't say anything more until they pulled into the driveway, and he shut off the engine.

"Look," he began, his hands still gripping the wheel. "I know this isn't any of my business, but maybe you should send him an e-mail letting him know how you feel. I'm not defending the guy, but he's not giving up. Maybe he just needs some closure."

She waited until Ron was finished talking before getting out. She heard him, but she didn't know how to respond. She already felt like she'd told Charlie enough. He should have thought about the kind of closure he wanted before he went and kissed Celeste.

Her mother ran out of the house and met her on the walkway leading to the front door. She was waving a large white envelope above her head. "Molly! Molly! This just came for you!"

She handed Molly the envelope. Right there on the front label was clearly marked CYNTHIA VINCENT.

In the past week Molly had completely forgotten about the internship. Her months of dreaming about it and the amount of work she had poured into her application seemed to completely vanish in light of recent events.

Pain like that tended to eclipse everything else.

She took the mail from her mother to be polite, but discarded it on the console next to the phone as soon as she walked in the door.

"Aren't you going to open it?"

Molly was already halfway up the stairs. "No, but you can if you want." She shrugged, resuming her way up.

A few minutes later there was a knock at the door. Molly was already lying down, staring up at the ceiling. Her mother entered, sat down on the edge of the bed, and reached over to run her hand through Molly's hair. In her other hand she was holding the white envelope.

"I know it hurts, Molls. And I know it feels like any sense of joy has been sucked right out of you."

Molly closed her eyes to trap the tears that started forming.

"But another thing I know is that you have a gift. And it's a gift that needs to thrive no matter who comes in and out of your life. This talent is yours, and no one can take it away from you. Not Charlie, or Celeste, or the internship committee, or even me. You have something to share with the world, and it would be a shame to throw it all away, with or without this internship."

Laura handed Molly some tissue. She wanted to embrace what her mom was saying, but there was a big gulf of despair preventing her from really believing it, or caring enough to open the envelope. Nothing seemed to matter anymore.

"Your father would be so proud of you too. You remind me of him, you know. Seeing the way you've devoted yourself to putting the application together and the way your face lights up when you're inspired. He was the same way when he was passionate about something, and he never swayed from his conviction, no matter who got in his way."

Molly was sitting up now. "I really remind you of him?"

"More than you even know."

Laura got up to leave and propped the envelope up against the elephant-shaped lamp on the pink nightstand between the two beds. "I'm going to finish making dinner. Take your time. Come down whenever you're ready."

Molly turned over and stared at the envelope. She wanted to open it, but there was something she had to do first. She got out of bed and walked down the hall, past the bathroom to Charlie's room. She took a deep breath and went in. Her laptop was right where she'd left it—and where it had been for most of the summer—on the unmade bed next to the pillows. She quickly retrieved it, trying not to notice anything else, and ran back to the twins' room.

She opened the computer, went straight to her e-mail program, and hit compose.

From: Molly
To: Charlie
Date: August 11, 2008 7:11 P.M. MST
Subject:

Dear Charlie:

I know what happened with Celeste. Please don't ask me how I know, but I do and there's no point denying it.

Soon we will be back in our respective homes and won't have anything to do with each other anymore.

All I ask is that you please respect my privacy. Don't call or e-mail
or try to reach me again.

Sincerely,
Molly

She didn't read the e-mail over or do a spell check or second-guess her
actions before sending it. She just pressed the button, and away it went.
Charlie was now officially out of her life. He got his closure. But instead of
feeling relief that she would no longer be nauseous for the hour leading up
to his daily call, or need to avoid her computer for fear of seeing his name
appear in her inbox, she felt worse.

She closed her laptop and reached for the envelope. It felt thick and heavy.
She opened it absentmindedly, like it was some dumb school newsletter she
would casually glance over and then discard.

She pulled out a glossy red folder. Inside, there was a typed letter on
Cynthia Vincent letterhead from the internship committee. After reviewing
materials from over five hundred extremely talented applicants they were
very pleased to inform her that she had been chosen as one of four finalists
and had an interview with the committee next week in L.A.

Molly returned the letter to the folder, which she stuffed back into
the envelope. She placed it facedown on the pink night table and went
downstairs for dinner.

I'll be the phonograph that plays your favorite / Albums back as you're lying there drifting off to sleep. . . .

—The Postal Service, "Brand New Colony"

Charlie rang Celeste's bell and knocked on the door. He had desperately been trying to track her down since receiving Molly's e-mail and had even checked her father's place a couple of times until he finally found out, through Jose, that she had gone to Paris and was due back today.

She finally came to the door in a robe. "What are you doing here?" It was the first time they had seen each other since the morning after the Farmers Market.

"We need to talk."

She stepped outside and closed the door behind her. "I just got back and I'm beyond jet-lagged so can this wait?" She acted different without her usual sexy clothes or makeup on.

"No, it can't." He had already waited long enough. "I don't know what you said to Molly, but you need to fix it."

"Excuse me?" Celeste said, genuinely confused. "I have no idea what you're talking about."

"I guess you also have no recollection of what happened the last time I saw you either." He was in no mood for her attitude.

"Yes, I remember." She looked down at her feet. "But what does this have to do with Molly?"

"You mean you haven't spoken to her?"

"No. She's been, like, a hermit all summer. What's going on?"

"Don't screw with me, Celeste," Charlie said. He hadn't considered the possibility that he was wrong and that Molly had found out what happened some other way.

"What's your problem anyway? You're, like, freaking out."

Convinced that she was telling the truth, Charlie filled her in on what was going on with Molly.

"HO-LY SHIT," she said, when he was done. "I can't believe it."

She didn't seem mad at all, but rather kind of shocked. "Don't sound so surprised," he said, suddenly a little defensive.

She turned to him and laughed. "No, it's just that you have no idea how huge it is that she even agreed to meet you in the first place. I mean, the Molly I know would *never* do something like that."

"Well, she didn't because somehow she found out what happened that night at the Farmers Market, and now she won't talk to me."

Celeste was quiet and reached for the doorknob. But instead of going inside she muttered something under her breath. Her back was to Charlie, so he couldn't hear her. "You have to speak up."

"I'm sorry," she said again, just loud enough so her voice was now audible. "It's all my fault."

Charlie softened. "You didn't know. I'm the asshole."

She still had her back to him. "I threw myself at you even though I knew you weren't interested."

She seemed to be crying now, because her shoulders heaved every time she took in a deep breath.

"I'm sorry I accused you," Charlie said. "Please—"

He moved to touch her shoulder, but she wiped her face with her sleeve and turned to face him. "I'll tell her what really happened. I'll help you get her back."

"Thanks, Celeste," he said, even though he knew that wouldn't be enough. Besides him, Celeste was the last person Molly would want to hear from. No, Celeste couldn't fix things. He had to fix them himself, and he suddenly had an idea how.

On his way down the steps he stopped and turned back. "You know, you don't always have to try so hard. People are still going to like you."

"Even you?" She looked at him in defeat, like she already knew he was going to say no.

"Yeah, even me."

All this while I've been packing ice around my heart. How do I make it melt?

—Ada Monroe, *Cold Mountain*

"I am so beyond relieved to see you." Molly jumped on one of two neatly made queen-size beds standing side by side and patted the space next to her for Rina to follow suit. It was pretty standard as far as hotel rooms went. "You're the only one who even knows I'm back."

She and Laura had just arrived in L.A. that afternoon and checked into the Biltmore for the night so Molly would have no distractions before her interview in the morning. Cynthia Vincent's studio was just down the street. The Richardses were still in their house, and Molly couldn't face going back until she knew Charlie was gone.

"Well, your secret's safe with me. Didn't your mom come with you?"

"She stopped by her office for a bit. I just ordered up pancakes and waffles from room service."

"Awesome," Rina said, fluffing up the pillow behind her. "So, how are you feeling?"

She meant about the interview, but Molly hadn't been able to stop thinking about Charlie. She had explicitly asked him to stop trying to contact her, but now that he was respecting her wishes, she felt a massive void. Here she was, in the same city as him, just a few miles away, but there was nothing she could do about it. "I think I'll be okay."

"You're going to do great. I know it."

"It's weird being here," Molly began. "I wanted to leave Boulder so badly, but now that I'm back, it feels even worse." One of the hardest things about leaving had been saying good-bye to Penelope, but she had promised to visit. She even missed Ron, who'd stayed behind to pack and do the key handoff when the Richardses returned. "I've barely been able to check my e-mail, because all of Charlie's messages are still there, and I can't bring myself to delete them."

"I have an idea." Rina got up, retrieved Molly's computer, and booted it up. "I'm going to clean out your inbox. There won't be any trace of Charlie when I'm through."

Molly felt a sharp pinch in her heart. "Delete them forever? I can't do that."

"Don't worry," Rina assured her. "There just won't be any trace of him in your inbox. They'll be on your hard drive; I'm just not telling you where, so at least you won't be cut off from civilization anymore."

"All right," Molly conceded, her heart rate returning to normal. "I can handle that. Just don't tell me how many there are."

Molly turned on the TV to distract herself while Rina began the process.

"Molls," Rina said a few minutes later, hitting mute on the remote. "There's one here I think you should read. It's from Celeste."

They still hadn't discussed what Molly should do about her former best friend. She'd been hoping to avoid the topic at least until after her interview. "I can't read it."

"I think you might want to hear what she has to say."

Molly folded her arms across her chest and closed her eyes. "You read it to me."

From: Celeste
To: Molly
Date: August 18, 2008 12:12 P.M. PST
Subject: PLEASE read me

M,

I just got back from Paris and found out about everything with you and Charlie. I had NO IDEA you two have been in touch and gotten so close. I really hope you read this, and I'm going to say everything really fast so I can get it all out. First, you have to know that NOTHING is or ever was going on between me and Charlie. That night at the Farmers Market was all my fault and a huge misunderstanding. I knew Charlie wasn't into me, but I got way too drunk and threw myself at him anyway on the dance floor. I don't know who told you what happened that night and I don't need to know. But you have to believe me that nothing else happened.

I love you so much and I would never do anything to hurt you. And Charlie's a wreck. It's obvious that he's so into you.

I needed you to know this and to understand why I haven't been in touch sooner. If not me, then at least give Charlie a chance.

Love,
Celeste

When Rina was finished she handed Molly a box of tissues from the bedside table. She waited until Molly had a chance to wipe her eyes and blow her nose before saying anything. "Maybe you should talk to him. Maybe you should talk to both of them."

Molly wished she could. "I don't know how."

She got up and walked over to the window. Staring out at the smoggy city below, she already missed the snowcapped mountains.

The magic of first love is our ignorance that it can ever end.

—Benjamin Disraeli

Charlie rapped the knocker three times and stepped back on the walkway, waiting for someone to answer. He didn't need a sign telling him "buzzer broken" to know that it didn't work. Not that he ever knocked or rang, since the door was never locked, except on Wednesdays, and it only mattered if he was the first one home after the cleaning lady left.

But for now it wasn't his house.

It was Molly's.

They weren't supposed to be back for almost another week, but his moms had finished their jobs. There was nothing keeping them in L.A., and they wanted to do this for Charlie. They were even waiting at a neighbor's so that he could see Molly alone, quietly, before they all descended on them.

Ron's Prius was parked in the driveway, which was a good sign. It had been a couple of minutes, so Charlie knocked again, louder this time, so that it would be heard even from the backyard.

"Coming!" a voice he recognized as Ron's called out. "Hi, can I help you?" He stood in the doorway, waiting for Charlie to say something, like he was a door-to-door salesman.

Ron was taller and thinner than Charlie had expected from his low, gruff voice. "I'm Charlie."

"Oh, I see." His response hung out there like a wet towel, like Ron already knew that Molly wouldn't want to see him. Charlie desperately wanted to look up at the window to his room, hoping that he'd get a glimpse of her peering out from behind the curtains, but Ron was staring right at him.

"I'm sorry I just showed up like this," he started to explain, trying to maintain hope a little longer. "It's just that I really wanted a chance to explain everything to Molly in person."

Ron sighed. "I seem to always be the bearer of bad news. You just missed her. She and her mother left for L.A. yesterday."

It took a second for it to register that she wasn't there. "Wait, that means . . . she got an interview?"

"That's right, she did." Ron smiled and considered Charlie for a moment before opening the door wider. "Why don't you come in? It's your house."

As weird as it felt knocking on his own front door, it was even stranger being invited into his home by someone he'd never met before. The house usually felt empty whenever they returned from a long vacation, like time had stood still while they were away. Everything was always exactly where they had left it, the house bearing witness to the stillness. But this time life had gone on inside despite their absence. Time hadn't stopped. If anything, it had sped up, and he could feel the difference just walking through the front door.

"My whole family's back. We decided to come home early. They're waiting at the Wilsons' down the street," Charlie explained.

"Tell them to come over," Ron said.

• • •

After dinner, Charlie went upstairs. The door to his room was open, and he stood at the entrance. It looked the same from that distance, everything seemingly as he left it, down to the *Star Wars* sheets, which were back on his bed.

He went over to the window to open the shades, revealing, in moonlit pools of light, the mountain peaks he loved so much. He looked down at the ledge, half-expecting Cheese to be sitting there waiting for him.

He turned on the lights and inspected the room, looking not for signs of misplaced items but for traces of Molly. Whereas the rest of the house brimmed with signs that other people had been staying there, his room was left empty and devoid of life. He kicked off his shoes and lay down on the bed. Pulling the sheets to his nose, he could smell Molly all over them, confirmation that she had once slept there. It was a fresh, subtle scent, like morning dew.

He stared up at the glowing galaxy on his ceiling, another sign that Molly had been there. Perhaps the only thing left to remind him of her.

There is no instinct like that of the heart.

—Lord Byron

"How'd it go?" Her mother leaped up from her seat in the waiting room and ran over to Molly as she came out the door. "You've been in there for almost two hours. Everyone else is gone."

"Good . . . I mean great," Molly said, still a little bewildered. "There were three people from her company asking me all sorts of questions, and I think they liked my answers, because at the end they took me to see Cynthia in her studio. It was unbelievable. She was right in the middle of designing the most gorgeous dress, and she stopped to talk to me for almost twenty minutes about how much she liked my portfolio."

"And what happened next?" Laura asked, hanging on every word.

"And then she offered me the internship. Right there, on the spot."

Laura pulled Molly in close and kissed her all over. "Molls! I'm so proud of you!"

It wasn't until they walked out into the bright Los Angeles sunshine that it hit her. She had done it—she had achieved her dream.

The other thing that hit her was that despite everything that had happened, there was only one person she wanted to share the news with—but she had to forgive him first.

Maybe she had made a huge mistake. Maybe she had been looking for a reason to cut Charlie out of her life; maybe on some level she knew she wasn't quite ready to face her biggest fear: getting her heart broken. But it had already happened, even if it wasn't anyone's fault.

No matter how hurt she was, she hadn't died or disappeared or even fallen apart. She was walking down the street, arm in arm with her mother, still happy.

"Let's go home," Molly suddenly said. Maybe it wasn't too late to get another chance.

"That's actually where we're heading. Ron called. The Richardses decided to return to Boulder a week early. They got there yesterday, so Ron's on his way home now. He should be here by dinnertime."

The tears sprang up before she could stop them. There were no more chances. Charlie was gone. It was really over.

"Oh, honey," Laura said. "Let's get you home."

• • •

Cheese was waiting for Molly when she got home. She opened the window wide, and he came rushing in to greet her. "I missed you, Mr. Cheese."

The room looked exactly the same, but she felt like a stranger in it. She had changed so much since she'd last stood there that nothing felt familiar anymore. She opened the dresser drawers, cleaned out, except for a single red shirt that had been left behind. She took it out and pulled it on over her dress. It wasn't Charlie, but it was the next best thing.

She had to face the fact that he was gone and there wasn't anything that could be done. The summer was over, and their real lives were about to begin. It was time to let him go.

But she couldn't. Whether they would ever see each other or not, she still had more to say.

She took out her laptop and began typing.

She must have been there for a while, because Cheese was gone, and it was dark outside when she heard someone knocking at her door.

She was so engrossed in getting her e-mail just right that she didn't hear the car pull up, the front door open, or even the footsteps coming up the hardwood stairs. She flung herself out of bed and ran to open the door. It had only been a few days, but she'd really missed Ron and was relieved he was home. She couldn't place exactly when it had happened, but she had gone from feeling resentful to really being grateful he had come into her life.

"I'm so happ—" She stopped mid-sentence, and stood motionless with her mouth gaping wide open. It wasn't Ron standing in front of her.

"Hi. I'm Charlie."

"You—you're here," she said, frozen in place. Despite the pages and pages she had just written, that was all she could manage to say.

"I'm here," he repeated. "I, uh, hitched a ride with Ron." He reached out and took her hand. "I'm here for you."

A rush of blood coursed through her body as she felt Charlie's smooth, soft skin. She was still trying to wrap her head around the fact that he was really there, in her room.

"Nice shirt," he said, breaking the ice. "Is that what you wore to your interview?"

She looked down at her ridiculous outfit and smiled. "Not quite," she laughed, tugging at the shirt she was still wearing over her dress. "You forgot this."

"I know," he said, smiling. "I left it for you."

His whole face lit up when he smiled, illuminating his bold green eyes. They were even more radiant in person, like they could see more than just what was in front of him.

Charlie pushed the hair out of her eyes. "I've wanted to do that for a long time," he said. "And this."

He leaned in to kiss her softly on her left cheek, then gently again on her right until he finally brushed his lips against hers.

Time slowed down to a halt. The room seemed to spin all around them, like it would never stop, the stars on the ceiling above glinting even in the fully lit room.

Molly wrapped her arms around him and pulled his body closer so she could breathe him in, so she could feel his heart beat.

"Meow."

They looked down at the exact same moment and burst into laughter. Cheese was underfoot, doing figure eights between them.

"Hey, Cheesy," Molly said, scooping him up. "Look who came back."

Charlie reached out to pet him. "I love you, Molly Hill."

She looked up, caught off guard. "What?"

He put his hands on her shoulders and looked directly into her eyes. "I love you," he said again.

Whether it was his touch or hearing those words or seeing him right there, in the flesh, she didn't know, but something broke inside her. *This* was her chance. She was getting her second chance.

Her instincts were telling her to go for it, that everything was going to be all right; they were yelling for her to let go and to open her heart the way Charlie was laying his open for her.

For the first time in her life, Molly realized, she was going to listen.

5/10   8   4/10

Acknowledgments

I would like to thank my editor, Kristen Pettit, for her keen insight and guidance, and for seeing the potential of this book before it was all on the page.

I'm indebted to Kate Lee for making it all possible, for her continued belief in my work, and for going beyond the expectations of any agent.

And thank you to Laura Schechter, for bringing it all home.

I would also like to thank my loyal readers, especially my mother, Dorothy Fieldman. Her artistic example set the mold. Many thanks also to Jen Ringel and Tom Vance for their astute comments.

Thanks also to Dave Rosner for his invaluable Boulder research.

A warm thank-you to Deborah Stern for helping me pave the way for this path, and to Aliza Pollack for her tireless support.

And finally, to my husband, Alex LeVine, for being such an avid listener with an open heart.